FLASHBACK

JUSTINE DAVIS

D0188244

Silhouette®

BOMBSHELL™

Published by Silhouette Books

America's Publisher of Contemporary Romance

If you purchased this book without a cover you should be aware that this book is stolen property. It was reported as "unsold and destroyed" to the publisher, and neither the author nor the publisher has received any payment for this "stripped book."

Special thanks and acknowledgement are given to Justine Davis for her contribution to the ATHENA FORCE miniseries.

 SILHOUETTE BOOKS

ISBN 0-373-51400-X

FLASHBACK

Copyright © 2006 by Harlequin Books S.A.

All rights reserved. Except for use in any review, the reproduction or utilization of this work in whole or in part in any form by any electronic, mechanical or other means, now known or hereafter invented, including xerography, photocopying and recording, or in any information storage or retrieval system, is forbidden without the written permission of the editorial office, Silhouette Books, 233 Broadway, New York, NY 10279 U.S.A.

All characters in this book have no existence outside the imagination of the author and have no relation whatsoever to anyone bearing the same name or names. They are not even distantly inspired by any individual known or unknown to the author, and all incidents are pure invention.

This edition published by arrangement with Harlequin Books S.A.

® and TM are trademarks of Harlequin Books S.A., used under license. Trademarks indicated with ® are registered in the United States Patent and Trademark Office, the Canadian Trade Marks Office and in other countries.

www.SilhouetteBombshell.com

Printed in U.S.A.

Praise for Justine Davis's *Proof,* the book that launched Athena Force

"Four stars. Justine Davis creates a capable heroine and a group of likeable, distinct characters. With *Proof,* she lays the groundwork for future books, with a well-paced, intriguing start to this ongoing mystery."
—*Romantic Times BOOKclub*

***

Alex studied the envelope for a moment.

The paper was heavyweight, rich feeling. It was addressed to her grandfather here at the farm, in a bold, looping hand that looked familiar. There was no return name or address, only an Arizona postmark.

She slid out the folded pages. A familiar letterhead stopped her dead.

"Marion," she murmured under her breath.

Alex fought off the instinctive shiver a communication from the dead gave her and read. And reread the letter, her shock growing. Finally she lifted her head and stared at her grandfather.

"She knew," she whispered. "She knew someone was trying to kill her."

Dear Reader,

When I got the information for writing the first Athena Force Bombshell book, *Proof,* I remember thinking, "Wow, I wish this place really existed!" What a great idea, an academy to teach women how to use their own unique talents to excel in a world where their success often comes only after a battle of one kind or another. I have personal experience with this; as the first female to step into what was once a male stronghold division of a local police department, I know what it's like to have people expecting—even hoping—for you to fail. If I'd been able to go to Athena Academy, I might not have been so worried about it.

Now the heroine of *Proof,* Alexandra Forsythe, is back for a new adventure, and I still feel the same way. As a next generation of fictional heroines-in-waiting join the ranks of Athena Academy students, I find myself both wishing it were real, and that I could have gone there myself.

But since it's not—yet—I will happily revisit the Athena world as Alex works to unravel one of the few threads left hanging after that first story, and finds that even the coldest of cases can quickly turn bombshell-hot!

Enjoy!

Justine Davis

JUSTINE DAVIS

lives on Puget Sound in Washington. Her interests outside of writing are sailing, doing needlework, horseback riding and driving her restored 1967 Corvette roadster—top down, of course.

Justine says that, years ago, during her career in law enforcement, a young man she worked with encouraged her to try for a promotion to a position that was at the time occupied only by men. "I succeeded, became wrapped up in my new job and that man moved away, never, I thought, to be heard from again. Ten years later he appeared out of the woods of Washington State, saying he'd never forgotten me and would I please marry him. With that history, how could I write anything but romance?"

Chapter 1

The satisfaction of a tight grouping in the ten ring on her shooting qualification was fading as Alexandra Forsythe sat cleaning her new Glock on her grandfather's front porch.

Charles Bennington Forsythe was rarely jittery. That he was now acting as if he'd been mainlining double espressos for hours was a fact not lost on his granddaughter. When he resorted to pacing the farmhouse porch, she couldn't hold back any longer.

"G.C.?"

Alexandra Forsythe used the nickname with affection and concern. As a child she'd made it up for this beloved man, who was more a father to her

than her real one had been, even before his un-
timely death. "Grandfather" had seemed too distant, and "Charles" far too lacking in respect. The
fact that G.C., her shortening of Grandfather
Charles, had made her mother wince was merely a
side benefit.

He kept pacing as if she'd not spoken, which
began to make her jittery in turn. Normally she would
not push him, having learned in her years as a
forensic scientist for the FBI that patience usually
paid off. But this was so uncharacteristic of him that
she found she couldn't just ignore his mood.

The afternoon breeze swirled her hair, and she
shoved red-gold curls back from her face. Determined now, she quickly finished up on the Glock, put
it back in the case, then got up from the cushioned
wicker chair that sat near the porch railing. She
leaned forward onto the rail, taking in the expansive
view of Forsythe Farms.

This was the place she loved most, the place she considered home, and of late the only place she found
peace. But peace was obviously not within her grandfather's grasp this afternoon, and neither, apparently,
was patience within hers. Not when G.C. was this edgy.

"You have two choices," she said without preamble.
"You can either tell me what's chewing on you or I can
go saddle Twill and he can beat it out of you."

She'd finally gotten his attention. He turned to
look at her, one corner of his mouth quirking.

"So, you'd like to see your old grandfather groveling in the mud, would you?"

As she knew from personal experience, the big bay hunter was a handful, by turns all heart or all contrariness as the spirit moved him on any given day. But her grandfather had been a horseman for decades, and there were few he couldn't handle.

"As if even Twill would have the nerve to toss you," she said, in exaggerated outrage.

He gave her that smile that had always made her feel as if she could conquer the world. "Only because you've taught him to trust."

"True. Now, if I could only get you to trust me with whatever it is that's bothering you," she said, looking at him steadily.

Her grandfather sighed. "I trust you," he said. "You know that I always have."

"But?"

"I'm not sure that what's bothering me matters after all these years."

She studied his face for a moment, saw the troubled look in his eyes and the furrow between silver brows that matched his still-thick mane of hair.

"It matters to you," she said softly. "So it matters to me."

His expression softened. "Inside with you, then. I'll tell you over lunch."

Their weekly lunch was a tradition Alex worked hard to maintain whenever she was at home. She'd gone through thinking she was going to lose her grandfather once before, and the awareness that he wasn't getting any younger rarely left her mind. She didn't like thinking about it, but there it was.

The only thing she thought about more was Justin. And that in itself bothered her. She wasn't sure how she felt about her fellow FBI agent, wasn't sure she wanted to feel about him at all. That he'd already assumed such importance in her mind was disconcerting enough.

But she couldn't deny she was tremendously attracted to him; he was good-looking without being pretty, confident without being cocky, and smart without being a smart-ass. He also seemed determined to make their relationship exclusive, and she didn't know if she was ready for that. She wished she could get him out of her head, at least for a while.

As was his wont, G.C. flipped on the noon news for background as they ate. No new disasters had struck the world, no one they knew had died, and the stock market had held steady. Alex had hopes this would cheer him, but then a clip of a politician flinging some charges G.C. strongly disagreed with set him off on a rant.

"He's an idiot. Most of them are, anymore. Hasn't been a decent senator elected since Marion," he muttered as long-time cook and housekeeper Sylvia Barrett set bowls of her homemade sorbet in front of them.

"Speaking of Marion," her grandfather began, then stopped. Finally he reached into his pocket and pulled out an envelope. Again he hesitated, enough unlike him to make Alex's concern rise again. But finally he handed it across the table to her.

"And this is?" she asked, still focused on him rather than the envelope she'd taken from him.

"I'd like you to read it yourself and tell me what you think."

Something in his tone and manner told her he was speaking to his granddaughter the FBI agent. This relieved her; she'd been afraid what he'd handed her was some sort of medical report she wasn't going to like.

She studied the envelope for a moment. The paper was heavyweight, rich feeling. It was addressed to her grandfather here at the farm, in a bold, looping hand that looked familiar. There was no return name or address, only an Arizona postmark, which made her frown. Her forehead creased when she noticed that the letter had been postmarked ten years ago.

Her gaze flicked to G.C., who sat across the table from her with an expression she couldn't read. He rarely used the mask honed by years in the upper echelons of power and the business world on her, and that he was using it now told her this was even more important than she'd guessed.

She slid out the folded pages. They were the same

rich, ragg-heavy paper of the envelope. When she lifted the the pages above the first fold, a familiar letterhead at the top of the page stopped her dead.

She knew now why the writing had looked familiar.

"Marion," she murmured under her breath.

She glanced at her grandfather again, saw that he was quietly, expressionlessly waiting. She looked back at the words handwritten on letterhead from the United States Senate, further labeled in the upper corner as from Arizona senator Marion Gracelyn. The list of committees she'd served on during her tenure as junior senator ran a considerable length down the left margin.

Alex fought off the instinctive shiver a communication from the dead gave her and read. And reread the letter, her shock growing. Finally she lifted her head and stared at her grandfather. She'd wanted a distraction, and she'd gotten one in spades.

"She knew," she whispered. "She knew someone was trying to kill her."

Charles let out a suppressed sigh. "I was almost hoping you'd see something different there."

She shook her head slowly. "It's…right here. Three accidents, that close together, that weren't really accidents? What else could it be?"

Charles nodded. His eyes were full of remembered pain as he gestured at the letter she held. "It's as if she's saying goodbye."

Alex looked at the letter again. Looked at the

closing line she had at first skimmed over in her shock at the other revelations the page held.

> I don't want this to sound like a letter from a foxhole, Charles, but I hope you know how much I love you and yours. We too often don't tell the ones we should, and sometimes we leave it too late.

He was right, Alex realized. She'd been focused on the warning implicit in the letter and hadn't recognized the tone of farewell until he pointed it out. Marion had not only known someone was after her, but had been convinced they were likely to succeed.

"What could have made her expect to be murdered?" Alex asked, forgoing the obvious next step, that Marion had been exactly right.

"More to the point, who on earth thought they could get away with murdering a U.S. senator?" Her grandfather's tone was grim.

And why hadn't this come out before now, all these years later? Alex wondered.

When Marion Gracelyn had been bludgeoned to death in a lab building on the grounds of her brainchild, Athena Academy for Women, it had been headline news for weeks. Speculation, both wild and informed, had flown around the country.

And if she'd been too young to know then, Alex certainly knew now what kind of pressure that type of high-profile case put on investigators. She'd borne the brunt of some of the frustration agents working such cases felt, when they wanted evidence processed immediately and everybody thought their case was more important than anyone else's.

She could only imagine what it must have been like after the murder of a United States senator.

So why hadn't this come to light? Why hadn't the investigators back then put it together? In all the digging she knew had to have been done, how had this been overlooked, the fact that Marion had known someone was trying to kill her?

Once more she looked at the second page of the letter, which held the short, stark documentations of the three events that on the surface looked like accidents or to the mystics, a string of Mercury retrograde bad luck. An automobile malfunction, a fire at her home and the crash landing of the small plane she'd chartered to make it to D.C. in time for a crucial vote.

Taken individually, Alex might have thought the same. But when you looked at them all together, she thought, took into account that they had all happened in the space of two months, and added the final, grimmest fact, that Marion had indeed been murdered, there was no way to see it differently.

And Marion had known it.

"Why didn't she tell me before?"

There was an undertone to her grandfather's voice, an almost plaintive note that made a long-ago and long-forgotten suspicion resurface in her mind, that her grandfather and the late senator had perhaps been closer than she herself had then been aware of. And something she'd at first skimmed over made her look back at the first page of the letter, addressed, she only now realized, to "My Dearest Charles."

She wondered, but she knew this was not the time to pursue that particular possibility.

"I don't quite understand, G.C. Have you had this all this time?"

"Yes and no," he said, his mouth twisting slightly. "I had it, but didn't know it. Obviously, from the postmark it came around the time Marion was murdered. Sylvia found it tucked away in the back of a drawer, under some linens. Our best guess is that one of the staff, knowing we were all grieving, put it out of sight to avoid causing more pain at that time, and then forgot about it."

And so it had languished there, hidden, for a decade, Alex thought. Only to surface now, when the case was as cold as a winter desert night at Athena.

"I suppose we need to step up the spring cleaning around here," G.C. said, but the quip fell flat. And since she didn't know what to say, Alex instead reread the details of the three incidents.

"She must have had some idea who was behind all this," Alex said, almost under her breath. "Why didn't she say so?"

"Marion was never one to make accusations

without having specific proof," Charles said, his voice level again.

Alex looked at him. "Do you have any ideas?"

"Obviously, her death wasn't at the hands of the casual burglar the police wrote it off to," he said.

"Obviously. But that leaves a host of other possible suspects, doesn't it?"

"Yes," Charles agreed. "Marion made enemies as both a prosecutor and as county attorney."

"And from what you've told me about her, some of them were near the top of the criminal food chain."

He nodded. "And some were people who had a great deal to lose."

"She took down a couple of politicians, too, didn't she?"

"Yes. Powerful ones. And it wasn't easy. In fact, that's why she ended up running for office, when she saw how much housecleaning needed to be done."

"Which means somebody with some dirt under the rug might not be too happy with her," Alex speculated, thinking that the list of possible suspects was growing exponentially.

"And then, of course, there's Athena," Charles said quietly.

Alex's breath caught. "Do you think it could be related to what happened to Rainy?" Alex and her best friends and Athena Academy classmates, the small, tight-knit group self-dubbed the Cassandras, had just gone through a nightmare of untangling a vicious-threaded mess of science corrupted and murder freely practiced. A nightmare that had begun with the loss of one of their own, Lorraine "Rainy" Carrington.

"It could have been, although the timing falls between when Rainy's eggs were harvested and her murder twenty years later. I think it's more likely that it's connected to Marion founding Athena Academy. Opposition to the academy was…virulent, in some quarters. And it was her brainchild, her vision that brought it to life."

Alex knew this. She'd always thought of Marion Gracelyn as a sort of unofficial aunt and a personal hero, but above all she'd been grateful to her for envisioning and making real the place that had changed Alex's life—and the lives of countless other women—forever.

Thanks to Marion, Athena Academy existed, and women had chances that had been denied them for so long, chances to make the most of themselves in whatever field they chose…as long as they could excel to meet Athena's stringent standards. Law enforcement, the military, science, athletics, whatever the discipline, it was open for Athena's students, and in the relatively short existence of the school her graduates were already proving themselves all over the world.

"The Athena Factor," Alex said softly, lost for a moment in the immensity of what Marion's dream had accomplished. She'd been hearing the phrase more and more, as the power brokers of the world ran into the results of an academy devoted entirely to the advancement of women without interference from misguided or antiquated views and glass ceilings.

"Yes," G.C. said. "But that's the very thing some powerful people were afraid of. Sad to say that some still are."

"Afraid enough to kill?"

Even as she said it, Alex shook her head ruefully. Of all people, she knew better than to question that.

"Just how bad was the opposition to Athena?"

"Startling," G.C. said. "Or at least it seemed that way to me."

"But you thought it was a good idea to begin with," she pointed out.

"Yes. I'd wished there was something like it from the time you were five years old and I realized what we had on our hands."

She blinked. "What you had on your hands?"

G.C. gave her the amused and proud smile that had warmed and encouraged her throughout her life. He'd made the absence of her late father so much more bearable, even through his own pain at having lost his beloved son.

"A girl who refused to see or set any limits," he said, "no matter what anyone said."

He didn't say it, he never would, but Alex knew he meant her mother, who had seemingly spent her life trying to rein in her rambunctious, redheaded daughter.

Girls don't do that was the phrase she remembered hearing most. She'd have been crippled by it if she hadn't been so stubbornly resistant, and if it hadn't been for G.C. countering her mother's negativity with his own brand of high-powered encouragement.

And, she had to admit, her brother, Ben, and his teasing that had goaded her on—intentionally, she later realized—to greater heights. If not for these things, she might have succumbed and become one of those women she had little use for, because they had little use.

Women like, sadly, her mother.

She jerked her mind out of that well-worn rut and back to the matter at hand. "What kind of opposition? From what quarters?"

Resting his elbows on the arms of his chair, G.C. steepled his hands in front of him and rested his chin on his forefingers. It was his pondering position, and as a child who adored her grandfather, Alex had long ago adopted it herself. She saw his eyes go distant, unfocused, knew he was remembering.

"Athena was truly Marion's brainchild," he said. "Her views on women's rights were well-known. So, many were surprised when she opposed opening U.S. military academies to women. But she knew what they'd be facing, that they'd have to fight so much harder than the men at those institutions did."

Alex nodded. "And it was hard enough for the men, without adding intimidation, harassment and the just plain not being wanted that women would face into the mix. I understand all that. But didn't a 'separate but equal' sort of solution placate those opposed?"

"You'd think so, wouldn't you? But we found that many simply opposed women being prepared for any part in what was then a man's world. Some almost violently so."

"And one perhaps murderously so?" Alex said softly.

G.C. sighed. "It certainly seems possible."

"Even probable." Alex shook her head. "Although it's hard for me to believe anybody could hate us that much."

"I'm not sure it's about hatred," G.C. said, "as much as hanging on to a tradition, a way of life that's all they know."

"So was the Civil War," Alex pointed out in a wry tone.

G.C. smiled at her as if she were an exceptionally clever student. "Point taken."

Turning her attention back to the letter, she held up the last page.

"What's with this?" she asked, pointing at the drawing in the lower left corner.

"I don't know," G.C. said, the tone of his voice telling her that he had spent more than a little time trying to figure out the meaning of the hand-drawn graphic that was almost cartoonish, yet at the same time quite ominous.

Only, she told herself, because it was a spider. A

big, fat one, crouched in the middle of a web made small by the looming body of the arachnid.

"All I can tell you," Charles said, "is that Marion was not a doodler."

Alex looked at the drawing again. "So…this isn't a casual scribble. It means something."

"It did to her," he confirmed.

Which meant it did to Alex, as well. Marion Gracelyn *was* Athena; it wouldn't exist without her vision and effort. And anything that threatened Athena or anything connected to it threatened Alex, because Athena was irrevocably entwined in her life and her heart.

As was the case for all the Cassandras. They'd renewed their promises to each other and to Athena in the aftermath of the investigation that had begun with Rainy Carrington's murder. She hadn't expected to have the call come again so soon, but apparently it had. And she would respond.

Any and every Cassandra would always rally to Athena.

Chapter 2

"So, what do you know about working cold cases?"

Justin Cohen blinked, then drew back slightly as he stared at Alex across the table and the remnants of their lunch. He was in town from Phoenix for a week of seminars he'd been sent to attend, but their schedules were so chaotic that moments like this when they both had a few minutes of free time were pounced upon somewhat rabidly.

"Probably not as much as you do?" he suggested, sounding puzzled at the unexpected question. "I mean, you're the forensics expert, and forensics is where more cold cases are broken than just about anywhere else."

Alex stirred her glass of iced lemonade with the straw. "I've gone over and over what's there, in our files. Nothing that led to a suspect at the time, but plenty to nail him once he's found."

His eyes—those stunning blue-green eyes whose image she'd been carrying around in her head since she was a teenager—narrowed.

"So you're talking about a specific case, not just cold cases in general." He didn't make it a question, but she answered that way, anyway.

"Yes."

"And a federal case, if we have a file on it."

"Yes. Federal because of who was involved."

"How cold a case is it, dare I ask?"

"A chilly decade or so," she answered.

"Hmm. Well, I've heard of worse. It's becoming more common as the technology advances. A guy I went through the academy with broke a thirty-five-year-old kidnapping case a couple of years ago."

"How?"

"DNA," Justin said. "But that was just the end result. He spent months before that talking to a lot of people, some of them old enough or sick enough that he had a lot of work to do sorting out what information was reliable. And going through every bit of paperwork and evidence with the proverbial fine-tooth comb. Over and over and over again. Until he found the guy to match the DNA to."

Alex's mouth quirked. "I was afraid of that."

"You?" Justin scoffed in disbelief. "You're not afraid of anything."

The response warmed her, but still she told him silently, Oh, yes I am. I'm afraid of you, how you make me feel.

She knew her reaction was over the top, but the logical side of her mind kept insisting she was nurturing a childish fantasy she should have long outgrown.

The Dark Angel.

The memory of Athena's midnight intruder, the boy the Cassandras had dubbed with that incredibly romantic nickname, kept getting in the way of her looking honestly at the man he'd become, who had so quickly become part of her life—mostly because he simply refused not to be.

But that boy, so passionately dedicated to finding out the truth about his sister Kelly's death back when Alex was still in school, had fired all their imaginations and been so deeply etched into her mind that…

It suddenly struck her that he knew more about cold cases than she did on a very personal level.

"You never gave up on your sister's case," she said. "You became an agent because of it."

He never liked talking about the reason he'd joined the FBI. She never doubted the death of his sister was the reason, but that kind of obsession was too Mulder-ish, he'd joked.

But she knew it was true. She knew he'd been driven, some even said possessed, so much that she'd been a little concerned about what would happen, what he would do when his quest was finally over.

And last year it had ended, as triumphantly as it could for him. But he seemed to have settled nicely into the life he'd carved for himself by sheer force of will and determination.

Perhaps in the process of his quest, he'd found his true calling. She hoped so.

After that moment's inner acknowledgment of his success, she went on. "Even when everyone told you there was no case, that she had simply died in surrogate childbirth, you kept on. For nearly twenty years."

He sat there for a long moment. Alex guessed he was thinking, as was she, of the huge, frightening mess his sister had been devoured by—the mess she and the Cassandras had recently exposed. Since it had directly involved Athena, the Cassandras had vowed not to stop until the truth was uncovered. When it finally had been, the ramifications were so broad she still had trouble taking it all in.

"That was personal," he said at last.

"So is this," she said.

"What? Your federal cold case is personal?" He seemed surprised.

"It is. It's connected to Athena."

"Isn't everything you do?"

His tone was wry, but he was grinning. Justin had come to know a great deal about Athena and the kind of women it turned out in the past year and a half. He knew what the school meant to all who attended, and Alex knew he'd come to appreciate the strength of the bond between the graduates and their alma mater.

"Yes," she said without embarrassment. "But this is different. It's not just the school. This has to do with the…creator of Athena."

His brow furrowed. "Allison's mother?"

He'd met Allison Gracelyn during the unraveling of the mystery surrounding Lab 33 and its genetic experiments, the motive behind Rainy's murder. Rainy had found out that the lab had used her for an experiment, back when she'd been an Athena student. And when her adult investigation had threatened to expose them, they'd killed her. Alex felt the usual pang the thought of Rainy, and how much she missed her, brought on. But she buried it for now; there was another Athena murder to unravel.

"Yes," she said. "Marion Gracelyn. Senator Marion Gracelyn."

His forehead cleared. "Ah. Hence the federal investigation."

She nodded.

"Didn't they determine she'd interrupted a burglar?" he asked.

"That's what they said," Alex agreed, her voice neutral.

"But you're not buying it."

"I never did," she said. "There was no reason an ordinary burglar would have broken into Athena."

He considered that for a moment. "Can't argue with that," he agreed. "It's too far out, too isolated, and there wasn't enough to steal—except maybe some hard-to-fence lab equipment and computers—to make it worthwhile."

She smiled, grateful he had so quickly seen the facts. His eyes widened, and she thought she heard him suck in a breath.

"Whatever brought on that smile, tell me so I can do it again. And again."

Alex fought down the heat that threatened to rise in her cheeks. He always managed to do that to her. He was so…blunt, sometimes, about how much he wanted her, and wanted her to feel the same way. It was such a change from Emerson Howland's cool, unaffected manner. It was taking her a while to adjust, to trust that it was real.

She pushed thoughts of her former fiancé away, along with any effort to respond to Justin's unexpected request. She knew she was going to have to quit putting it off soon, but now was not the time. She had too much on her plate right now.

"There's new evidence," she said.

He seemed reluctant to accept the change back to the original topic, but at last nodded at her to go on. She told him about the letter. And again he wasted no time with trying to explain things away.

"So she knew someone—or maybe plural—was

after her. And those supposed accidents were just failed attempts."

She nearly smiled at him again, but stopped in time; she wasn't ready for another round of dealing with his ardency just now.

"Exactly," she said.

"How long's the list?" he asked.

"Of suspects? Lengthy. I was thinking I'd start with the ones here."

"Here? You mean in D.C.?"

She nodded. "There are a few of them who didn't want to see Athena even exist, let alone succeed."

"Which it has, and then some. It's a force to be reckoned with these days."

Athena Force. The new nickname they'd chosen for their expanding group of crime-fighting Athenians echoed in her head. The warmth of belonging to such a stellar group—and of having Kayla, one of her closest friends—back in her life, filled her.

"Given the circumstances and that a lot of those people are still here, that's where I'd start," he said.

"But?" she asked, hearing the unspoken qualifier in his voice.

"In the end, I think most cold cases are solved at the scene, or in the place most closely connected to it." He shrugged. "That's why I kept going back to Athena over and over again after Kelly died. It was the only connection to her death that I was sure of."

She'd already had the feeling that she was going

to end up back in Arizona. It all seemed to come back to that. As before, Athena seemed at the center of the storm. Marion had to have known she'd be stirring up things when she'd begun the academy for young women, but Alex wondered if she'd ever imagined just how much. Or how far and for how long the ripples would spread.

So, she'd be going back. She hadn't expected to be investigating another murder so soon, but when it came to her beloved school she'd do whatever had to be done. Any Cassandra would.

"Anything I can do to help?"

At Justin's words she snapped back to the present. She appreciated the offer, but this was Athena, her home and her problem. Or theirs, she amended. She figured she'd end up calling on some of her fellow Cassandras before this was over and done. And Allison, of course. She was first on the list.

But she'd leave the door open, she thought.

"Not yet," she said.

He nodded as if he understood.

And perhaps he did, Alex thought. He seemed to understand a lot. Perhaps it was just his innate knowledge and acceptance of the concept of loyalty. She knew he had it; the man had spent half his life pursuing the truth about his sister's death. They'd been closer than most siblings, the barely legal Kelly having fought hard to keep her teenage younger brother with her after their parents had died. And

Justin had never lost his determination to see through the last and only thing he could do for his beloved big sister.

Would he be that dedicated and loyal to *anyone* he loved?

She brushed away the question she wasn't sure she wanted answered just yet. But she was going to have to deal with it soon. They were growing steadily closer, and she was going to have to make up her mind just how close she wanted to get to this man who was both a teenage dream come to life and a threat to her adult peace of mind.

But for now she had to focus on Athena. And a decade-old murder.

"I've moved on, Ms. Forsythe. Long ago."

Was there a bit of extra emphasis on the Ms.? Alex wondered. Was that General Stanley's way of releasing a lingering distaste for what, at the time, he felt had been forced upon him?

It made no sense, really. Marion had been one of the military's greatest supporters, and to kill her over something like this would be an exceptionally grievous case of cutting off their own nose.

She pondered her next words. She'd taken the week off work, hoping in that time that she could at least get a feel of how difficult investigating Marion's death was going to be. She'd already made a flight reservation to Phoenix for a couple days from now, based on what Justin had told her, so she was pushing to either clear the people who were here in D.C. or pry a direction to look out of one of them.

"How do you feel about Athena now, sir?"

She made her tone respectful, both because of his two-star rank and because she wanted answers more than she minded giving a verbal bow to the man. She had tremendous admiration and respect for the military—"land of the free because of the brave" summed it up for her—so it wasn't difficult for her to speak carefully to this veteran.

"If you're looking for a rash quote to spatter across the front pages, you'll have to go elsewhere," he said.

He sounds defensive, she thought.

"Why would you think that?" she asked, still careful to keep her voice level.

"Because you're a graduate of Senator Gracelyn's invention."

She hadn't mentioned that, but she supposed it wouldn't take a genius to figure it out. And she couldn't help but notice that for someone who insisted he'd moved on, he certainly seemed touchy about the subject.

But what she noticed most was that despite his obvious feelings about Athena, he referred to Marion Gracelyn by her proper title and with the respect it was due. That, and her gut was telling her this man hadn't been involved. She'd learned to trust her gut.

"If you feel so strongly about it," she said, not caring quite as much now about being tactful, "why did you agree to see me?"

The man in uniform leaned back in his chair. "You can't live in this town for very long without learning that antagonizing a Forsythe isn't wise, no matter who you are," he said bluntly.

An image flashed through her mind of a dinner her grandfather had hosted a couple weeks ago, at the gracious Alexandria home he'd built for his late wife, Alex's grandmother. Alex lived in the house now, as much as she lived anywhere other than her job and the farm.

But she'd absented herself that night, intentionally; she didn't have the clearance required to be present given the guest list and some of the topics that would be discussed. It had been a small gathering inside, but the number of secret service men outside spoke volumes about the attendees.

No, in this town Forsythe was not a name to take lightly. The name was a weight Alex was always aware of, although she preferred her grandfather's style to her mother's more pretentious, self-aware version.

"No," she admitted, with a grinning, inward salute to G.C., the man who'd so quietly built the Forsythe name into what it was, "it's not. But I thought perhaps it was the FBI on my ID card that convinced you."

"We try to cooperate with all federal agencies," he said stiffly, "but although you're an agent, you did say your visit was…unofficial."

Which, Alex nearly said aloud, was akin to having a reporter say you're off the record. "It's personal," she acknowledged.

"You writing a book or something?"

"A book?"

"About the founding of that school of yours?"

Not a bad idea for a cover, actually, Alex thought. "Everyone else in this town seems to be," she said.

"Yeah." An inelegant snort accompanied the tone of disdain. "So, if your question is did I support the senator's plan, the answer is no. It was too late. We'd already been forced to open up the established academies to women. I didn't see the point."

Alex went back to her earlier question. "And now?"

"Hasn't done any harm," he said, and to his credit there was a minimal amount of grudgingness in his voice.

But still, Alex thought, faint praise. She'd be upset if she didn't know the truth. Athena tracked alumni well after graduation, and she'd seen the figures comparing their success to that of women who hadn't had the advantage of an Athena education. The difference was nothing less than remarkable. Athenas consistently went higher faster than any others, living proof of the validity of Marion Gracelyn's vision.

But part of that vision had also been maintaining

a low profile. Drawing less attention was one of the reasons Athena was a college prep—grades seven to twelve—and not a university. Athena's goal was to empower women, not gain glory for itself. It didn't rely on fund-raisers or tax dollars, and so didn't need a high profile to curry favor and cash. Which explained why many still didn't know of its existence, or that the difference they were seeing in the number of women raising the glass ceiling and earning influential positions these days was because many of them were Athena graduates.

Alex thanked the general, noted he didn't try to crush her hand as she stood and shook his, and moved him down toward the bottom of her list.

She didn't take him off it. She wasn't taking anybody off at this early stage.

Her afternoon appointment netted her an endorsement from a senator she wouldn't have expected it from. Patrick Rankin, Junior Senator from New Hampshire, told her that he'd only opposed the school for political reasons, that he himself had always thought it would work.

This was a surprise, because the man was an ally of senate lion Eldon Waterton, who had been an Arizona senator since long before Marion was elected. Waterton had opposed her on nearly every matter, although he'd stayed out of the Athena issue.

G.C. had always suspected that it was because he had a granddaughter he hoped might attend someday.

Politicians, he grumbled, were all for standing on principle for everybody else.

As Alex barely managed not to gape at Rankin, he went on to say that he was glad he'd been proven right, that Athena women were shining in all fields. He seemed a bit too curious about why she was asking, but she also couldn't help but notice that his statements were peppered with comments that revealed a certain admiration for Senator Gracelyn. Or perhaps it was simply courtesy to a fellow senator.

She moved him farther down the list as well.

Not that I won't put you all back on top if necessary, she said to herself later as she wearily kicked off her shoes in the foyer of the Alexandria house.

The second her bare feet touched the floor the phone rang. She considered not answering since she was so tired, but a glance at the caller ID told her it was Justin. She was answering before she even realized it.

"How'd it go today?"

"Just got home. I'm afraid I haven't had the proper appreciation for you field guys," she said.

"Well, that's certainly true." She could almost see him grinning, could almost see the dimple that slashed into his right cheek when he did.

"People complicate things. Forensics, physical evidence, is…not simpler, but cleaner somehow."

"It doesn't lie."

"Exactly. And it doesn't try to hide. If you can't

find it, you're just not looking hard enough, or in the right place."

"Welcome to my world," he said. "You sound a bit weary of it all."

"I am," she admitted. "Exhausted."

"People will do that do you," he said, sounding annoyingly chipper. "But since you have the grace to admit that you've underestimated us field grunts, I'm going to reciprocate."

"Reciprocate?" she asked, puzzled.

The door chimes rang—they were loud, to be heard throughout the large house—and drowned out whatever his answer had been.

"Hang on," she said, "there's someone at the door."

"I know."

"You know?"

Boy, I am tired, and apparently confused as well. He's not even making sense to me, she thought as she walked back to the front door, glad she hadn't sat down yet; she wasn't sure she could have gotten up again.

"I know," he repeated as she peered through the security peephole.

"Oh."

She felt beyond silly. Not even the fish-eye lens of the peephole could totally distort Justin's dark good looks. She pulled the door open to the sight of him standing on the porch, cell phone in one hand and a large bag in the other.

"Cute," she said, disconnecting.

"I thought so."

His smile was irresistible. "Not that it's not good to see you," she said, accepting the kiss he planted somewhere between her cheek and her right ear, "but...what are you doing here?"

He flipped his cell phone closed and held up the bag in his other hand. "Dinner. Chinese okay?"

The smell had hit her nose by then, a lovely, warm barrage of soy and spice and sweet, and her stomach lurched hungrily.

"Bless you," she breathed fervently.

"I thought you might be glad not to cook tonight."

"I'm always glad not to cook," she pointed out as she stepped back to let him in.

"And I'm glad to let you," he retorted, ducking her halfhearted swipe at him.

"I have other skills," she said as she snatched the bag from him.

The familiar white cartons were stacked high, topped by a pile of napkins and plastic utensils and emitting those luscious aromas that made her stomach growl in anticipation yet again. She barely managed to stop herself from burying her face in the bag just to get a deeper whiff.

"Indeed you do," he said. "And I hope to sample them all someday."

Alex was glad she had her back to him, although she didn't need to see his expression to know what it looked like. Not when his voice had gone so dark and smoky all of a sudden.

The Dark Angel speaks, she taunted silently, trying to chide herself into a cooler response.

It almost worked.

But then he stepped up behind her, put his hands on her shoulders and bent to gently kiss her neck. The shiver that went through her warned her yet again what she was likely in for should she ever—perhaps inevitably—give in and sleep with the guy.

Holy fireworks was all she could think of.

"I'm reading an awful lot into the shiver that just went through you," Justin whispered.

That dark angel voice nearly made her shiver again. "I suppose saying I got a chill won't work."

Her irritation at herself for being unable to control her reaction to him echoed in her voice.

"Not a chance," he said, his voice still soft, his breath still warm and making her skin—and other things—itch. She barely managed not to squirm, he was so close.

She twisted and ducked away from him. "Just what were you figuring I tipped for food delivery?"

He made no move to come after her, merely stood watching her with an expression she could only describe as amused. In a tone that sounded just as amused, as if it were the middle of some casual conversation, he said, "I'm very patient, you know."

Alex swallowed tightly. She knew that. He'd waited

years to get the people who had murdered his sister. She'd just never quite applied the knowledge to their personal situation before. And now that she had…

She was going to lose this battle, she thought. He would wear her down with that damnable patience of his. She'd hold out a good long time but in the end she would lose.

She tried not to hear the little voice that seemed to emanate from the tightness low and deep inside her saying that in this case, losing meant winning.

Chapter 3

As usual when she needed to think, Alex retreated to Forsythe Farms and the back of a horse.

"I hear you're writing a book."

Alex blinked, startled. She reined her horse in as she stared at her grandfather. "Well, that didn't take long," she said.

"I have my sources," he said blandly.

"Don't I know it," she said, remembering the times when he knew about her college escapades before she'd even returned to her dorm room. She'd always been aware he seemed to know things—even trivial information—before anyone else, but she hadn't quite expected this to get to him this quickly.

"I assume that's your cover, for those who don't already know you're with the FBI?"

She nodded and nudged Silk forward again. The cream-colored filly was aptly named; her gait was as smooth as her coat. As was her disposition. Even the fidgeting of the temperamental Twill, in an exceptionally feisty mood this evening and only grudgingly bending to her grandfather's experienced hands, didn't seem to phase her.

Her calm temperament was unusual for such a young horse, and Alex suspected they had a real treasure in the making. It was horses like this that made her sometimes wish she'd stayed in this world and pursued her riding career. But she knew she wouldn't trade the challenges of her job for anything, and that moments like this she could steal would have to do for now.

"General Stanley guessed that that was what I was there for, and I sort of let him go on thinking it. It seemed like a decent cover. Although he did say to pass along his thanks to you, for always being there for the military when they need you."

G.C. nodded. "What little I can do these days. But we'll stick with the book story for now. I suppose being rather well-known here could make things difficult."

"It's a handicap and a benefit," she said. "I get in to see higher-ups more easily, but those higher-ups know more about me than I'd like for this purpose.

It affects what they're willing to tell me. I think I may do better in Arizona, where I'm more anonymous."

"You've called Allison?"

"Yes. I left a message since she was out. I didn't say it was urgent, since we're just starting, but I thought she should know."

Twill snorted and danced as a dragonfly darted in front of them. With practiced ease G.C. brought him back in line. Silk shook her head when the insect came too close to her nose, but otherwise remained calm.

"Learn from your daughter," G.C. told the big bay stallion in mock sternness.

It was a minor chastisement directed in jest to an animal, but Alex couldn't help thinking how the words he'd said demonstrated one of the things she loved most about her grandfather. Despite his position and the importance others assigned him, he never thought he was too big or too important, never thought he knew too much to ever learn from anyone around him.

They finished their ride, untacked and groomed the horses under the hovering eye of head groom Jacob Garner. Garner, even after years of working for the Forsythes, had never quite gotten used to their penchant for taking care of their own horses. He'd even told her once that it was a topic of discussion among other grooms in the area, how unusual it was that the Forsythes insisted on doing such things themselves instead of just handing their horses off to staff as most others in their circle did.

It wasn't until they were walking from the stable back to the house that G.C. returned to the subject of her investigation.

"Will you be talking to the police in Phoenix? Asking them to reopen the case?"

"Officially? I'm not sure yet. I'll talk to Kayla, certainly, and maybe the detective assigned the case if he's still there."

Her beloved Lacy, registered name Chantilly Lace, whinnied at her from the paddock where she was enjoying the spring day. She laughed, and changed direction.

"She'll never forgive me if I don't take her out soon."

"Jacob says that tendon is healing nicely, so a little ramble shouldn't be out of the question by next week."

Alex nodded, glad the horse she'd grown up with since she was a child was doing better. She didn't push her so hard anymore, now that she was in her twenties, but Forsythe horses were long-lived and spirited, so she expected to be out on the trails with Lacy again soon.

After the horse had been greeted and cooed over and seemed satisfied for the moment, they resumed their walk up to the house, and the conversation.

"I'd like to do as much as I can under the radar," Alex said. "Less warning, and less time for the roaches to scurry into hiding."

She was certain Kayla Ryan, her friend and fellow Cassandra, who was now a lieutenant of the Athens

Police Department, would have some ideas on how to proceed. And knowing Kayla, she'd be off and running herself once she found out what Alex now knew from Marion's letter.

Alex felt no hesitation about letting Kayla in on what they'd found out. Despite the rough patch their friendship had been through, she had never questioned Kayla's loyalty to Athena. And she didn't question it now, or that Kayla would be eager to start digging the moment she heard.

"And I suppose professional courtesy requires that I let the locals in Phoenix know that I'll be poking around," she went on, thinking aloud now. "I don't want to use the book-writing cover story with them only to have them find out later I was scamming them. I might need their cooperation before this is over."

"Spoken like a woman brought up around politics," he told her.

"Yuck," she said succinctly, making an exaggerated face of distaste as she knew G.C. expected. She won the grin she was after; her grandfather knew quite well her aversion for the world he held so much power in, despite the fact that he had never run for or held public office.

"That feeling you have is why Marion ran for office," he said.

Alex shook her head. "I admire her for that. I think. My first thought about a filthy pond is how to clean it without going swimming in it."

He looked at her with an amused expression. "And how would you do it?"

"Drain it?" she suggested. "Then shovel the dregs out into the compost pile and start all over with clean water."

He chuckled. "You'd be amazed at how many people agree with exactly that idea. Too bad more of them aren't in positions to do it. Yet."

The rest of the evening, except for a brief phone call from her mother—brief because Alex escaped by saying she was busy preparing for the trip to Athena—passed in the pleasant manner that made her long for this place when she was gone. She was so relaxed and calm by the time her grandfather said good-night that she was startled when he added soberly, "Be careful, Alexandra."

"Of course," she responded automatically.

But as she lay awake that night, turning things over in her mind, she wondered what he thought might happen in Arizona, what had compelled him to issue that caution about a case that was a decade old.

It might be a decade old, a small voice in her head pointed out, but it was still murder.

And the murderer was still out there.

"I can't believe Jazz is old enough to be at Athena," Alex said.

Kayla Ryan laughed. "Neither can I."

"She's doing quite well already."

Christine Evans, the only principal Athena had ever had, or had needed, spoke enthusiastically as she handed the two other women glasses of the lemonade she'd just fixed. They'd both chosen it rather than wine, knowing they'd be driving later tonight.

They'd wanted to meet here, not just because they loved Athena and came back often, but also to check on Christine, and make sure she was truly completely recovered from the gunshot wound she'd suffered during their unraveling of Rainy's murder. It seemed that she had, and Alex knew that yet another Athena class would be whipped into shape by the indefatigable ex-army captain.

That class was here now and was the main reason Alex was staying in town instead of out here at the campus. With a new session of school in full swing, Alex hadn't wanted to intrude on the rhythm, even if Christine had said she wouldn't be at all in the way.

"Jazz has some awfully big footsteps to follow in," Alex said, nodding at Kayla, whose honey complexion pinkened in what Alex guessed was pride more in her daughter than herself. But her brown eyes sparkled, much as Alex guessed her own blue ones did at the happiness of having her closest friend back in her life.

"A little mother-daughter competition won't hurt her."

"I'd argue that," Alex said ruefully, "except you are thankfully nothing like *my* mother."

"And Jazz can't, and shouldn't, be me." Kayla grimaced slightly. "Hopefully she's smarter than I was at her age. She's her own person, and she'll have to find her own path, her own talents."

"And Athena's the place to do it," Alex said, shifting her gaze to Christine, "thanks to you."

"My, you're just full of praise tonight," Christine teased.

"Maybe I'm just glad to be with people who love Athena as much as I do."

"Uh-oh," Kayla said instantly at the undertone Alex hadn't meant to let show in her voice. "Problem?"

"No, not really. Not a current one, anyway. But I do have some news."

She filled both women in on why she was there, and both were, as she'd expected, as eager as she to get to the truth about Marion Gracelyn's murder. Christine spent quite a bit of time walking Alex through every bit she could remember about that day.

"Did Marion ever tell you anything about those three incidents that happened before she was killed?" she asked Christine.

Christine frowned. "I knew she had that fire at her home here in Phoenix, the one that they thought was arson, and then, of course, that awful crash with that plane that ran off the runway when taking off."

"And a week before that, the steering on her car went out," Alex said. "Her mechanic said the fluid was contaminated. Something that gummed up the works. He wasn't sure exactly what it was. Highly unusual but not unheard of."

"Well, yes," Christine said. "I heard about that, but…you're saying they're all connected?"

"Marion thought so."

"The fire *was* arson," Kayla put in. "I remember looking up the report shortly after I started at the PD, when I had access to old reports."

Christine looked thoughtful. "It does seem a bit much to have three 'accidents' of that severity in such a short time span. I should have…I just never put them all together that way."

"You were in shock," Alex said. "Everybody who knew and loved her was in shock, not thinking clearly."

"So you think those accidents were failed attempts on her life?"

"I pulled the NTSB report on the plane accident. The official verdict was accidental debris on the runway, but there were two dissenting investigators who thought it might have been intentional damage done to the plane's tires."

Kayla drew in an audible breath. "So if we accept that these were all caused incidents, we're down to who caused them."

"And if we can figure out who caused them, it should lead us to who killed her," Alex said. Then she looked at Christine. "Did you have any suspicions, at the time it happened?"

"I never thought it was someone who'd been against Athena," Christine answered. "Not that there weren't plenty of them. But Athena already existed, and was successful, by the time Marion was killed. Why would anyone wait that long?"

"I tend to agree," Alex said. She knew that Christine had excellent instincts about people, and a great deal of common sense.

"Judging from what I've heard around town over the years," Kayla offered, "it could just as easily have been some conspiracy freak, with a crazy idea about what Athena is. People still have some out-there theories."

"I guess I hadn't realized," Alex said, "that so many people had such wild ideas about us."

Christine chuckled. "It's the price we pay for the low profile. When people don't know exactly who or what you are, they either don't care or tend to make it up for themselves. And most people who make it up have outrageously over-the-top imaginations."

"Tell me about it." Kayla's tone was wry. "When I applied at the PD, and they found out I went here, the first thing one of the old farts on my oral board asked was if that was the school that taught women to take over the world and drive men out."

"Good grief," Alex said. "What did you answer?"

"I said no, but that it did teach us to recognize men whose masculinity was so fragile they were afraid of strong women, and how to treat them gently."

As Christine laughed, Alex hooted aloud; she'd never heard that story from Kayla before. "And yet you still got the job?"

Kayla grinned. "Turned out they dragged out the old dinosaur for every female's entrance exam. Figured if she could deal with him without getting rattled or angry, she had a chance of making it."

"Sounds like a good plan," Alex said.

"It is," Kayla agreed. "And come to think of it, the idea came from Eric Hunt. The detective who handled the investigation, although he was still the dinosaur's partner when I came on. He was Phoenix PD then, but he's ours now."

"What's he like?"

"He's a cop," Kayla said, as if that said it all. As perhaps it did, Alex thought. But then Kayla added, "A good one."

Alex waited, sensing there was more but not wanting to push. At last, with a sigh, Kayla went on.

"He's just in a rough place right now. Tired. A string of tough cases and long hours. He's liable to be a little touchy at first, that's all."

Alex nodded. "I'll be gentle."

Kayla laughed. "Don't be. Eric doesn't need it. As long as he knows you're not there to make cops look bad, he'll help you."

"You know that's not why I'm doing this, right?" Alex asked. It was an aspect that hadn't occurred to her before Kayla had mentioned it.

"Of course I know," Kayla said. "But it's him you have to convince."

"I'll manage."

"You always do," Christine put in. Then, settling back in her chair, she eyed Alex with interest. "So...tell me about you and the Dark Angel."

Alex nearly groaned. "Can't we stick to something easy, like ten-year-old murders?"

It was Kayla's turn to laugh. Alex quickly turned on her friend; anything was fair game now. "Why don't we talk about you and Peter instead?" she said, referring to the detective Kayla had gotten involved with during Rainy's murder case.

"Because he's not an Athena legend," Kayla said with exaggerated blitheness.

"Fine," Alex said, defeated. "He's fine. I'm fine. We're still testing the waters, trying to make the long-distance thing work."

"Wasn't he supposed to be in D.C. about now?"

"Yes." She tried to leave it at that, but Kayla and Christine were both watching her too intently. "He is in a D.C. Training seminar. We'll be getting together when he gets back here."

And if I weren't the biggest coward on the planet, I'd probably be staying at his place, like he'd offered, instead of a hotel.

Later, she tried not to fixate on the thought as she headed back to her nice but impersonal room at that hotel. Justin had been great about not push-

ing for more than she was ready to give, while at
the same time making it clear that he wanted more.
Much more.

Not that she didn't want it, too. She was
just…what? Cautious? Careful? Wary?

Afraid?

She didn't like the idea, but she couldn't defini-
tively say it wasn't true. She was honest enough with
herself to admit it, even to figure out why. It annoyed
her that she was letting her mother influence her, but
it was an example she'd had all her life.

But she knew she couldn't drag it out forever.
Either they were in a relationship that would by def-
inition have to progress, or they weren't. Justin was
tacitly giving that decision to her, telling her that his
was already made.

He'd also understood her need to dive into this investigation, and accepted easily her leaving for
Arizona so soon after he'd left it for D.C. He was
going to be busy most of the rest of the week,
anyway. He'd simply changed his schedule to come
back when he was done, instead of hanging around
there an extra few days to spend them with her.

She wished she wasn't so confused about her
feelings. There was more to it than the fact that she'd
barely escaped what she was sure would have been
a disaster with her former fiancé, Emerson. She just
wasn't sure what it was. While her maternal grand-
parents and her parents had had a rocky relationship,

G.C.'s had been solid and happy until her grand-mother's death, and that was what she thought of when she thought of such things.

And while she'd been relieved to end her engage-ment to Emerson, she hadn't been wary of marriage itself. Not that she was sure that was what Justin had in mind, of course. Nor was she sure how it would work out if it was. Not with careers that had them currently living with most of the country between them. Twenty-three hundred plus miles was at the upper end of geographically undesirable.

The only thing she really was sure of was that Justin wouldn't wait forever.

Alex shivered.

She had to be having a flashback to the last time she'd been here, when they'd been trying so desper-ately to disprove the assumption that Rainy, their beloved Rainy, had fallen asleep at the wheel and died in the ensuing accident. Why else would she feel a sudden chill, despite the fact that the temperature was a balmy, Phoenix-in-spring seventy-two?

She pulled the rental car into the left lane to pass a slow-moving gardening truck. Someone behind her had the same thought and also pulled to the left. She glanced at the truck as she passed, noting the lawn-mowers in the back, and wondering about the people who insisted on having a lawn in this climate.

She smiled at the driver as she passed, silently

congratulating him for managing to make a living at being an anachronism.

She eased back into the right lane so she could make the turn up ahead that would take her to the Athens Police Department. As she went, she resumed mentally running through the contents of Marion's letter. She had it virtually memorized by now, both intentionally and from repeated readings, including last night at the hotel.

She'd left the original with her grandfather, who was going to keep it safe just in case. She'd thought it wise not to carry a copy of the letter around with her, so she'd made a list of the high points in an encrypted file on her PDA.

She slowed her speed after she completed the right turn. Building was going on here at a mad pace, as it seemed it was everywhere in the greater Phoenix area, and she wasn't sure she'd spot the driveway she needed in time to make the turn.

Sure enough, the vacant lot next to the police station, that area of scrub and mesquite that had always been her landmark, was no longer empty. The big marquee for the new convenience store nearly obscured the small sign for the department, and she almost missed it.

A quick glance in the mirror told her she had enough room between her car and the blue sedan behind her to make the quick turn. She heard some hard braking farther behind her, and silently apologized to the driver of the gardening truck, who was now pulling over to the curb, probably to re-secure something that had come loose because of her quick move.

She found a parking spot in front and was quickly out and heading for the front steps when she remembered she'd left her PDA in the car. Since it had all her notes in it, including those on Marion's letter, she turned to go back for it.

And stopped dead, staring.

She blinked, but she knew she wasn't mistaken. The blue car that had been behind her was stopped in the convenience-store parking lot. The vehicle was still running, dark-tinted windows closed. Angled so the driver could see the police department building, and the spot in which she'd parked her rental.

She recognized it now as the car that had pulled out from behind the gardening truck at the same time she had. As if the driver had seen her spot him, the car suddenly reversed out of the drive, tires squeal-ing. The car rocked as the driver hit the brakes. She heard the bark of tires biting as the car accelerated hard and fast, cutting back into the traffic lane, nearly clipping an SUV that was driving decorously along in the slow lane.

In moments the blue car was out of sight.

Coincidence?

She couldn't be sure, but she didn't think so.

What she did think was that she had the answer

to that chill she'd felt before. On some level she'd been aware of the car's presence.

On some level she'd known she was being followed.

Chapter 4

"Just what I need, a fed."

Alex caught the muttered imprecation, although she doubted she'd been meant to. Detective Eric Hunt—Kayla had introduced them and then sneakily decamped—looked up quickly, as if he suspected he'd spoken too loudly.

He'd be nice looking, she thought, if he ever smiled. There was something appealing about his boy-next-door looks, sandy hair and golden-brown eyes. He seemed...trustworthy, she thought. A good quality in a cop.

"Look," he said, "I know you're a friend of the lieutenant's—"

"Don't let that influence you."

He gave her a look that told her what he thought of that piece of impossibility.

"Just," she said lightly, "think of me as a P.I."

She smiled. He frowned.

"A P.I.? With an FBI badge?"

"This has nothing to do with the FBI. I'm investigating an old case of yours, yes, but as a private citizen."

She supposed she couldn't blame him for the suspicions that showed in his expression. In his place, she'd be hard-pressed not to wonder herself.

In his place, she thought, I'd get some sleep.

He looked beyond tired. Beyond even exhausted. He looked, she realized, burned out. She'd become familiar with the look, that world-weary, heard-too-much, seen-too-much expression that could quickly collapse into don't-give-a-damn. Once somebody hit that wall, coming back was a long, hard road many chose not to even attempt.

He leaned back in his chair. It creaked, the way just about every government chair she'd ever seen did. His cubicle was typical, small but not cramped, plastered with notices and suspect photographs, official memos and reminders.

But not, she noticed, much in the way of personal items. A postcard with a photograph of a snowcapped mountain, a snapshot of what appeared to be that same mountain and, looped over a pushpin, a long chain with a set of dog tags. She couldn't read the name from where she stood.

"How long have you been a cop?" she asked.

His frown deepened. She guessed if she'd been anybody else the answer would have been "What's it to you?" Instead it was a grudging, "Eighteen years."

Long enough to burn out. And then some. "First job?" she guessed. He didn't look over forty, even with the tired eyes.

"Yeah. Straight into the academy from college." He shrugged. "All I ever wanted to be."

He still sounded a bit on edge, so she tried another tack.

"Just so we're clear, I don't expect anything from you. I'm not asking that you reactivate the case or get involved at all. I'm just letting you know I'm here, and what I'll be doing."

"What do you want, then?"

"Your thoughts about the case, mainly. And a look at the original file. I've seen ours but not yours. Although, if you have any personal notes or recollections, copies of those would help, too. Beyond that, I'll stay out of your hair."

He leaned back slightly, puzzlement replacing the frown on his face. "Why?"

She lifted one shoulder. "Because, this is personal, not official."

"Oh? You guys took over the case in the first place,

the vic being a senator and all, so why don't you check with your own investigators?"

"I have. But you were first investigator on the scene. Your impressions are the most important."

"So I'm supposed to believe an FBI agent—"

"Scientist."

"Whatever. I'm supposed to believe the FBI shows up in tiny little Athens asking about the unsolved ten-year-old murder of a former U.S. senator, and it's only personal, I'm not going to get sucked up into the federal wood chipper?"

Her mouth twitched. She fought the grin. "It is a bit of a stretch, isn't it?"

She finally got the smile she'd been thinking about earlier. And it did, as she'd suspected it would, transform his face. He went from guarded and world-weary to open and approachable—and charming—in the space of a few seconds.

"It really is personal," she assured him. "Marion Gracelyn was a longtime family friend. She was like an aunt to me, and my family would really like to know the full truth of what happened that night."

"Wouldn't we all," Hunt said wryly.

"It means even more to me, because of where it happened."

He lifted one sandy brow. "The women's academy? You go there?"

"I did."

He looked curious then. "I hear it's quite a place. Lieutenant Ryan went there didn't she?"

Alex nodded. "She did. We were best friends."

"And she's one of the best cops I've ever worked with."

"I'll tell her you said so," Alex said with a smile.

"Oh." He looked chagrinned. "I guess you already knew that."

"We were in the same class," Alex said. "So yes, I know how good she is."

No point in trying to explain about the Cassandras; he didn't need to know, and likely wouldn't understand anyway. Nobody would who hadn't been in that kind of situation where the bonding was deep and permanent.

Whether it was that she knew Kayla, curiosity about Athena or something else, she didn't know, but he came over to her side after that.

"Look, your guys pretty much nudged me out of the whole investigation once they got here. Not that I blame them, really," he added in a burst of refreshing candor. "I was pretty green."

"Sometimes I think I still am," she commiserated, and earned another smile.

"Naw. Definitely red," he quipped, and to her surprise she didn't mind the reference to her hair. Perhaps it was the boy-next-door thing that softened it from taunt to friendly tease.

"Anyway," he said quickly, as if he'd embarrassed

himself, "most of the files of that era aren't digital, so they're in storage in Phoenix. I can send for them, but it'll raise a flag."

She knew that was likely true; you didn't dig out a murder case on a U.S. senator without drawing attention.

"I could tell them it's just been bugging me, and I want to look at it again," he said.

Something in the way he said it told her it wasn't totally a ruse. "Does it? Bug you?"

"Yeah," he admitted with a half shrug. "It does. It was my first murder, and probably the biggest case I'll ever be involved in."

She nodded in understanding. "Well, I'm not really trying to hide what I'm doing, just to keep it under the radar as long as I can. So if you think you can do it without sending up a flare…"

"I think so," he said, and she smiled at the change in his attitude. Oddly, he glanced away for a minute, much as she did when she thought she was going to blush.

"Thank you." She put every bit of sincerity she was feeling into her voice. "I really appreciate it."

As if inspired by the positive reception of his first offer, he said "I can dig out my own notes, if you think it would help. I kept all the old ones on paper, so it's not a digital file." He gave her a slightly sheepish smile. "And back then, I wrote down *everything*."

Definitely boy-next-door material, Alex thought.

"So did I," she said, grinning at him. "I think it would probably help a lot, then. Thanks, Eric."

He colored visibly then, and grinned back at the same time, a combination she thought awkwardly sweet.

It seemed she had gained an ally.

"Anything else, Agent Forsythe?" he asked.

"Alex," she said, granting him the familiarity she'd already taken. She started to answer his question in the negative, then thought again. "Could you have a license plate run for me?"

He looked surprised, but nodded. "Sure."

She handed him the piece of paper she'd scribbled the number from the blue car on. He took it and sat down at the computer terminal on a table behind his desk. Less than a minute later he handed her a printout.

The name and address meant nothing to her, but she hadn't really expected it to. She tucked it away, just in case, while he dug into the bottom drawer of the big file cabinet that stood beside the desk. While it was in the back of the very full drawer, he had no trouble finding the file, and Alex guessed it was because he looked at it with some regularity. As did most cops with the cases they couldn't forget.

He straightened, glanced inside the dog-eared and marked-up manila folder and then held it out to her.

She opened the cover, scanned the first page of neatly written, single-spaced notes. "Are you sure you don't want to just make me a copy and keep the originals?"

"I'd just as soon you had to bring them back," he said.

Her gaze snapped back to his face. Had she interpreted that right?

He gave her a one-shouldered shrug. "You brighten up the decor around here," he said.

"Thank you," she said, a little taken aback. But he didn't press any further, and she was left not certain if he'd meant it as merely an aesthetic comment or an invitation.

He walked with her back to the front of the department. As they neared the doors, Alex held back. "Would you do me a favor? Look out and see if you see a medium-blue sedan with very dark tinted windows parked anywhere within line of sight?"

"The license plate?" he guessed.

She nodded. Without further questions he walked over to the doors and stepped outside. After a couple minutes he came back inside. "Don't see him. But if you want, I'll open the back gate for you, and you can get out using our employee exit. Maybe a pile of marked units will make him think twice."

"Thanks," she said, meaning it as much for the fact that he hadn't asked her any questions as for the escape plan.

As she pulled out of the rear parking lot, drawing

some curious glances from uniformed personnel, she was relieved to see no sign of the blue car there, either. Perhaps it really had been a coincidence. But once again she had to admit, there were times when her distinctive curly red mane of hair was a definite drawback.

In case it was not a coincidence—and she was inclined to go with her gut reaction that it was not—she headed back to the hotel by a different route than she'd come by. She had Eric's personal notes in her satchel, and her plan for the afternoon was to settle into her room and go over them inch by inch. It would take a while; he hadn't been kidding when he'd said he wrote *everything* down.

But that could only help her in her quest for anything that would mesh with the new information she had from Marion's letter. Hopefully, he would have the original case file by tomorrow, and she could plow through that, hot on the heels of the notes, and everything would mesh together.

At her hotel room door she had to shuffle her load of satchel and the lunch she'd picked up on the way—a fast-food drive-through purchase that would have made her mother faint dead away—to insert her card key again. And again.

Nothing. No blinking green light to signal the unlocking of the door.

With a sigh she looked around, spotted the courtesy phone in the elevator lobby and headed that way. She called the desk and explained her problem.

"I'm so sorry, Ms. Forsythe. Let me just check something here…."

There was a pause that went on a moment too long, and Alex's antenna for trouble snapped up,

"Is there a problem?" she asked.

"Well…I…we thought you had checked out," the young male voice said, sounding nervous.

"Checked out? I just got here, and my reservation is open ended."

"I know, but…let me check this note on the file…here it is, it says you had to return home unexpectedly. A family emergency."

Alex went cold, the chill weakening her joints and making her skin clammy.

"Who gave you that information?"

"Um…it doesn't say." The young voice sounded even younger, and very worried now. "But I'll send someone up right away with a new key."

"To a new room. And send someone with a clue about how this happened, please." She realized she had sounded very sharp, and tried to ameliorate it. "I realize this is not your fault, but I need to know how and why this happened for…other reasons."

"Very good, Ms. Forsythe." The voice seemed calmer then, and Alex hoped that would result in answers to her questions sooner.

But first she had a much more important question that had to be answered immediately.

She yanked out her cell phone and hit the voice-activated key. She had to rein herself in to say "G.C., home," in a tone the phone would understand.

The five rings before his voice mail picked up seemed to take forever. She left a hasty message and hung up to try the private line to his home office; if he was busy there he often didn't answer the house line.

No answer again.

Damn this age where we all have so damned many phone numbers, she thought as she tried his cell phone.

It went immediately to voice mail, telling her he was either on it or it was turned off. He always turned it off at home or in meetings, she told herself. Or when he simply didn't want to be reached, wanted to, as he put it, slip the electronic leash. She left another message.

Her hands were shaking now, and she took a deep breath to steady herself before her last chance. She apparently didn't do that well, because the phone didn't recognize her voice command on two tries. She canceled the effort and hit the speed-dial button to dial her grandfather's office in the city.

She held her breath until his assistant, Ruth Epson, answered.

"Ruth? It's Alex."

"Hello, dear! How are you?"

A normal greeting, Alex thought, her hammering pulse slowing a bit. "Fine, but in a bit of a rush. May I speak to my grandfather?"

"Oh, he's not in today, dear. He has that meeting with the FTC, remember?"

She did, suddenly. There was a Federal Trade Commission hearing coming up, about a proposed new tax structure on textiles, and her grandfather, as usual, had been called upon to explain the facts of the industry to those ignorant of it.

"Have you seen or spoken to him today?" she asked Ruth, who had been G.C.'s right hand for twenty years.

"This morning," she said, relieving Alex's worries a bit more. "He called to pick up messages before he went to the meeting."

"Did he seem…all right?"

"Why yes, he seemed fine. His normal self. Why?"

Well, she'd done it now, she'd managed to spark that note of worry in Ruth's voice. She tried to lighten up her voice.

"Oh, nothing really. I think I just had a joke played on me, about G.C., but I had to make sure, you know?"

"Some people just have sick senses of humor," Ruth commiserated.

"You would know, you've been in that city long enough," Alex said, and was gratified to hear the woman laugh. She herself was feeling a bit better, although she wouldn't relax until she'd talked to G.C. herself. "If you hear from him, please ask him to call me as soon as possible. Or if he can't get free, would you call me and tell me you've heard from him?"

"Of course I will. You're really concerned, aren't you?"

Alex tried to soothe the woman's own motherly concern. "I just worry about him. He means the world to me."

"Ah, child, as you do to him. I'll make sure you either talk to him or I'll let you know when I have. Don't you worry."

Alex said goodbye as she heard the elevator doors open. A woman in the tailored blazer of the hotel staff hurried toward her, already apologizing. Behind her was a bellman with a suitcase and carry-on bag that looked very much like hers.

"I just don't understand," the woman whose name tag read Lynn said. "The man had your room number and reservation code."

"Man?"

"Yes." Lynn consulted a piece of paper in her hand. "He called at 10:00 a.m., from out of state, and said you'd had to come home immediately. That you'd asked him to call and handle this because you'd be on a plane."

"Did he give you a name?"

"No, but he identified himself as your brother."

Ben?

Alex's heart picked up speed again; was there really an emergency after all? Had he been hurt, injured? Was he in trouble? Or was it Tory? She knew her brother and her fellow Cassandra were involved with each other. In fact, it had been Tory Patton who had strongly hinted to her that Ben wasn't merely the scapegrace it appeared he'd become, relieving somewhat her constant worry about her beloved brother.

Still, she hadn't thought of contacting him. Her focus had been on G.C., not her brother. She wasn't even sure where he was at the moment.

Heck, you're not even sure who he is *at the moment,* she muttered to herself.

"He said to pack up your things carefully," the woman went on, "and that you'd send someone for them later."

So those *were* her bags on the cart, she thought. And this was rapidly moving from the arena of sick joke or harassment to carefully thought-out plan. And that made her very nervous.

"Again, I can only say we are so very sorry for the inconvenience."

"I have a feeling it was totally out of your control," Alex muttered.

"What can we do to make up for this unfortunate mixup?" Lynn asked.

"I would like another room, please, on a different floor. But I need to get into this one first, to make sure nothing was overlooked."

"Of course," the woman agreed immediately. "And if you find any damage to anything in your luggage, the hotel will be responsible."

I'm not the lawsuit type, Alex thought, realizing

the woman was working hard to make it right and avoid anything unpleasant for her employers. But right now she just wanted to get this done.

Lynn unlocked the door, and Alex cautiously stepped inside. The maid had apparently already been in, the towels were fresh and the bed was made. The drapes were nearly closed, the slight gap letting in a swath of light that fell across the table beside those windows, as if it were a spotlight highlighting the one thing in the room that looked out of place. A single page of newspaper, with a ragged edge that told her it had been torn out.

"I don't know how they missed that," Lynn said, taking a step toward it.

"I'll get it," Alex said hastily, stepping ahead of the woman. She paused only to look at the door itself; the lock appeared intact. She bent to look and saw what appeared to be a small amount of some kind of smeared residue on the faceplate of the lock.

She reached into her purse and took out a latex glove from the small packet she always kept handy. She pulled it on her left hand and touched the edge of the residue. The glove clung for a moment, then released. Whatever it had been, an effort had been made to clean it, which had probably destroyed any evidence value.

Lynn was staring at her, but she wasn't about to take time to explain. She entered the room, and after a quick look to be sure she wouldn't be disturbing anything else, she reached out for the torn newspaper page. When she got to the new room, she'd pull out an evidence envelope to put it in, and keep from disturbing any trace evidence or prints that might be on it. At least it was porous paper, and more likely to retain prints.

She wished she had her own lab equipment handy, or even just a lab to borrow, but she knew any good forensics person would find anything that was there.

Then she saw what was on the page, the story that had been highlighted by the way the page was folded, and her heart slammed into her throat.

She stared down at the small but painfully clear picture of the man who had been at the center of her life for as long as she could remember. And couldn't deny what was right in front of her. The threat was implicit, just short of declared in black-and-white.

The story was from yesterday's paper, about the upcoming FTC hearings, accompanied by a photo of her grandfather, exiting the Federal Trade Commission Building after a meeting last year.

The very same building where he was meeting with them today.

Chapter 5

Although she knew it was relatively quick, it seemed like forever before they had arranged a new room. On the concierge level this time, no doubt as part of their effort to placate her, because they had no way of knowing that this little inconvenience was the very least of her current worries.

She was anxious to get started on trying to contact her brother and coming up with alternative means to try to confirm G.C.'s whereabouts and health. She just managed to stop herself from shooing the anxious woman and the bellman out of her new room. Only the memory of her mother's imperious manner in doing such things made her speak gently.

"Thank you very much, this is fine. But if you don't mind, I have a lot of work to do...."

Alex didn't think it was her imagination that both of them grabbed at the chance to decamp. Must have been the sight of the latex glove, she thought.

With an effort she slowed herself down and secured the piece of newsprint first, sliding it into an evidence envelope she retrieved from her traveling kit. She made herself not look at it again, knowing she had to focus.

Then she grabbed her phone again and dialed the only number she had for her brother. He'd told her that, because he traveled so much, it made sense to just keep a cell phone. For a long time, Alex had thought that his true reason for the cell was that he was never sure which bimbo he'd be with when, but now that he was involved with Tory, that was hardly likely. No man alive could keep up with more than one woman if that one woman was Victoria Patton. And not simply because she was a star reporter rapidly rising to international reknown.

She smiled despite her worry. She'd once wished that Ben would run afoul of an Athena woman, just so she could watch the fireworks. She'd had no doubt who would win, and that it would probably be the best thing that could ever happen to him.

And now that he had, and the Athena happened to be Tory, she was even more sure that it would be the best thing. If he didn't blow it. If he hadn't forgotten how to be a genuine good guy during all his running around after women all over the planet.

Of course, if anybody could straighten him out, it would be Tory. And not the least of Alex's enthusiasm was based on the fact that if they married, having a woman who was like a sister to her as a legal sister of sorts, would be a lovely situation.

"Don't blow it, bro," she muttered as his phone rang. And rang.

It finally went to voice mail, an invention she was beginning to hate. Even the recorded message wasn't Ben's voice, but just a stock announcement of the number she'd reached. She left a message that she hoped sounded urgent but not panicked.

She thought for a minute, decided this was too important not to pursue all avenues and called Tory. After a brief exchange of pleasantries and updates, she cut to the chase.

"Is my brother with you?"

"No, I'm at work," Tory said, sounding puzzled.

"Have you seen him today?"

"Umm…"

Alex had been so focused on the situation from her end, and her desperation to make sure G.C. was all right, that she hadn't realized what her question implied, given who she was talking to.

"Tory, right now I don't care if you're having wild, monkey sex with him, I just need to reach him."

"Whoa."

Yikes, Alex thought at Tory's odd tone of voice. Maybe the monkey sex was really happening. She'd give a lot to see the look on the green-eyed, black-haired beauty's face right now.

"Uh…I saw him this morning," Tory finally said.

"Was everything all right?"

"Fine. What's wrong, Alex?" Tory asked, her quick reporter's mind seizing on the urgency Alex was trying to hide.

"I'm just trying to unravel a nasty joke," she said. "Do you know where he is now? He's not answering at his cell number."

"He said something about a meeting," Tory said, "but I don't know with whom or where."

The sex must be really good for Tory to turn off that inquiring mind of hers, Alex thought, and then grimaced. She knew her brother was undeniably sexy to women, but he was still her brother and she didn't want to dwell on his sex life. Especially given that she was fighting her own battle in that arena of late.

Thanking her friend, Alex hung up while wondering why on earth she was so stubborn about sleeping with Justin when everybody around her seemed to be having a fine time, sexually.

She was going to have to address that, and soon. Enough hiding. But first she had to resolve this immediate situation.

She put the phone down on the table and stared out the window for a moment, trying to fight off the memory of that shaft of sun spotlighting that ominous piece of newspaper, left carefully arranged so that it would be one of the first things she'd see when she came back into the room.

Something else hit her then. How had whoever it was known she would even see it? Wouldn't the logical thing for her to do be to go directly to the new room, unpack her bags and see if anything had been overlooked then? How had they known to place that article there, how had they known she would insist on going back to the room herself?

She didn't like the implications, but she put her misgivings on hold for the moment. G.C. was her first priority now, and until she knew he was all right, nothing else mattered. But she wasn't sure yet how to handle this veiled threat without causing more fuss than she wanted just now.

There had to be a way to verify he was okay. None of the Cassandras were in D.C. at the moment, so they couldn't help. Involving her mother, the perennial overreactor, was out of the question. And she could hardly ask Sylvia Barrett, who hated the city, anyway, to drive all that way from the farm and then make the trek through tourist central.

Ruth? A possibility, although if she did that she'd have to give her all the details, and she wasn't sure she wanted to send the woman into a situation when she didn't know all the ramifications. Especially since whoever was behind this, whatever it was, obviously was aware of things going on in D.C. and so possibly located there.

So she needed someone who could handle the unexpected. Who knew enough about D.C. to get around and along, depending on what they encountered.

Jim Hernandez, head of Forsythe Mills security maybe? He could—

The obvious answer finally flashed through her mind, in what she called a "Well, duh!" moment.

Justin.

"You're an idiot," she told herself as she grabbed up her phone. She'd have to analyze this sooner than she thought, so she could figure out why she was so wary of letting this man have what he'd made it so clear he wanted; to be part of her life.

"Cohen."

"Hi. It's Alex."

"Alex! Hi!" His pleased tone made her feel worse for not thinking of this sooner.

"Are you in the middle of a session?"

"No. Lunch break."

"Quantico?" That would make things difficult; the FBI facility was forty-five minutes away from the National Mall.

"No. Hoover."

She let out a relieved breath. FBI headquarters, the famous Hoover Building, was only three blocks from the FTC office. He could walk it easily, a good idea along always-congested Pennsylvania Avenue.

"How much time do you have?"

"Ninety minutes." His voice changed. He'd clearly sensed there was more than casual interest in her inquiries. "What do you need?"

It was an effort not to just blurt it all out in an emotional rush. When it came to her beloved grandfather and a possible threat to him, her professional composure was hard to hold on to.

"I need you to go to the FTC."

The pause was brief enough to make her grateful. "And?" he asked.

"My grandfather's supposed to be in a meeting there. Something's…come up, and his phone's off, and he's not answering my page."

"The Apex Building? Three blocks up Pennsylvania?"

"Yes."

"Okay. Give me a minute to make a call and I'm on my way."

Obviously he was changing lunch plans. No questions asked. Alex felt a tug inside, a combination of warmth and something else even stronger, something she didn't have time to dwell on right now.

But she realized she'd better tell him a bit more about what had happened, so he'd be prepared. Just in case. She gave him a quick-and-dirty version. And again he was right there with her.

"I'll make my phone call on the way," he said, quickly adjusting his plan in response to her urgency.

"And I'll call you back as soon as I lay eyes on him. Do you want him to know?"

Bless you for understanding that, Alex thought. "Not unless it's necessary."

"All right."

To her surprise she realized she felt no need to elaborate. She trusted his judgment on when it might become necessary. She wasn't sure she'd ever trusted anybody outside of Athena that much. Not with G.C.

"Thank you, Justin," she said, letting every bit of the emotion she was feeling into her voice.

"You should have called me right away," was all he said.

After they'd disconnected, Alex sat there nearly shaking in relief. It was a new feeling for her, to have someone besides G.C. and her sister Athenas to depend on. It was also a new feeling for someone who had fought for and prided herself on her independence for so long. It had never occurred to her before, that perhaps she'd gone too far in that quest for self-sufficiency. That in her quest for that independence she'd shut out the rest of the world. That perhaps it wasn't so bad to occasionally lean on someone.

That it was a man who made her knees wobbly was a side issue she'd have to deal with eventually.

Well, maybe sooner than eventually.

Calmer now that she'd know about G.C. soon, she called Kayla.

"Hey, girlfriend. Eric being helpful?"

"Yes," she said. "He's going to have the original file pulled out of storage, hopefully without raising any red flags."

"I got the feeling you wanted a low profile, so I stayed out of it. I wasn't even here then, so I thought my asking for it might raise an eyebrow you didn't want raised."

"Thanks," Alex said, "you're absolutely right. But something else has developed."

"Oh?"

"A threat, of sorts."

"What kind of threat?"

Alex heard the sudden sharpness in Kayla's voice, the sudden protectiveness in her tone, and smiled inwardly. It was so good to have her dear friend back in her life. And it seemed only natural when she found herself pouring out every detail of what had happened.

"Anything I can do?" her friend asked as soon as Alex had finished.

"Everything's on hold until I'm sure my grandfather's all right."

"I understand," Kayla said quickly. "Shall I make some inquiries at the hotel?"

It was on the tip of her tongue to say no, she'd take care of it. But the revelation she'd just had about her own independence stopped her. Sometimes she literally couldn't do it all herself. She had someone she could trust; she should accept the offer.

Not to mention that it couldn't hurt to have the weight of Kayla's local badge behind any questions asked. Besides, she had a lot of reading to do here.

"Would you?"

"Of course."

Kayla sounded both surprised and pleased, confirming to Alex that perhaps she had gone a bit too far on the independence front. She had the feeling this might be behind the impression others had told her she gave off, of being aloof. Just perhaps she'd gone all the way into stubborn.

Like G.C., she thought with an amused quirk of her mouth as she again disconnected her call.

As it had all her life, anything that pointed out similarities between herself and her grandfather made her proud.

A memory hit her with vivid clarity then, of herself as a child, expressing to her grandfather her disappointment in not being a boy. He had immediately and forcefully rebuffed the notion.

"Women," he'd told her firmly, "have traits and talents men would do well to emulate."

"Like what?" she'd asked, doubtful despite the fact that her heart and head told her he had to be right, simply because he always was.

"The spirit of the tigress, slow to rouse but implacable once enraged. Empathy, which can lead to understanding one's enemy, a necessity for victory. The ability to subordinate honor to getting the job done, a problem that has caused many a male-led mission to fail. And that's just for starters."

She hadn't realized until she was much older that these were hardly the words of the simple business-man he called himself. And while he'd never talked about it, and had often refused any discussion of it, she suspected he'd been involved over his years in D.C. in many things other than the textile business.

"One of these days you're going to tell me," she said aloud, refusing to think that she might lose him before that ever happened.

Refusing to even consider that she might lose him because of something she'd done.

Chapter 6

When she heard the phone across the room ring, Alex was so deep into reading Eric Hunt's exhaustive notes that it took her a split second to pull herself out of them. The man had clearly considered every possibility, no matter how unlikely. And he had documented each of those theories in his personal papers, even if they had been discarded or proved wrong later.

He had, she had to admit as she put down the pages of notes, thought of things that hadn't even occurred to her, and as she read she gained a new respect for the man's skills and thoroughness.

As Kayla had said, he was a good cop.

She got up to answer the phone call, glancing at

the watch sitting beside the telephone, the watch she had made herself take off so she would stop looking at it constantly, counting every second that passed as she waited to hear from Justin.

It was the front desk, calling to inquire if everything was all right with her new room, and to apologize profusely again for the inconvenience and ask if there was anything else they could possibly do for her.

She had barely hung up when the phone rang again. This time it was Lynn, the manager, and the anxious tone in her voice told Alex that Kayla had already been busy.

"No, there's nothing official in the way of an inquiry or investigation," Alex reassured the woman. "Lieutenant Ryan just happens to be a concerned friend, that's all."

"She did explain that to me. But she also seemed to indicate this was…personal? That this wasn't just a prank of some kind?"

"No, it wasn't a prank. It was aimed specifically at me and mine. So it's clear it's not the hotel's fault." She tried to relieve the woman's concern, since she needed her cooperation. "There's no way you could have stopped someone intent on committing this kind of act."

"We appreciate your understanding," Lynn said, relief clear in her voice.

"But you can obviously see why I'm concerned

about how this was done, in particular how whoever did this knew what room I was in."

"Of course. I spoke to the bellman who packed up your things, and he said he found nothing unusual or amiss in the room."

Alex fought down the distaste she felt at some stranger, even a hotel employee, pawing through her personal things, even just to pack them up. Odd, she thought. Her mother reveled in having such chores done for her.

Of course, her mother wasn't an FBI agent. Thank goodness she'd had her weapon and travel evidence kit with her, along with anything else of a sensitive nature, all secured in her satchel.

"However," the manager confirmed, drawing Alex's attention back swiftly, "the maid who went in to clean the room—which we only did of course because we believed that you wouldn't be returning—said she did have a brief conversation with a man out in the hall. She said he was only asking directions to the health club."

"She was cleaning my old room?"

"Yes."

"Could she describe the man?"

"Actually, she's at the police station with your friend right now. Something about a composite picture?"

She should have known Kayla would run with it, Alex thought.

"Thank you," she said.

"Is there anything else I can do?"

"Just make sure that no one except the people on the list I gave you has access to my room number."

"Oh, the staff has strict orders, I promise you. We'll do whatever is necessary to ensure the rest of your stay is pleasant and there are no further incidents."

Alex hung up and began to pace again, something she had only managed to stop when she'd forced herself to take out the detective's file and concentrate on it. It had served as a distraction, but her worry about G.C. was never far from the surface, and it took only moments before she was as revved up as she'd been when she'd first realized the threat.

This time she glanced at the bedside clock. It had been nearly forty-five minutes since she'd hung up with Justin. Give him ten minutes to extricate himself from the building, ten more to thread his way through the crowds to the FTC Building, she thought.

Then he'd have to go through security and the ID process there—they took few chances there like any other federal building—and find the meeting. That could take another twenty. Then—

Well, she wasn't sure what he'd have to do then. But he was likely doing it now. She'd just have to trust him and be patient.

Patient.

It had been the bugaboo of her life, of her career.

What she had of patience had been hard learned and hard won, and by now she was convinced it would never come easily to her.

She remembered a ceramic plaque her fellow Cassandras had once given her, with a cartoon of two very hungry-looking vultures on a branch, waiting for something to die so they could eat it. The caption showed one bird saying, "Patience, hell! I'm going out and killing something!"

It had been funny, and it still held a place of honor on her kitchen wall, standing out among all the flowery plates her grandmother had favored. But she understood the feeling all too well. She still did. She hadn't grown out of it in the years since. She was used to making things happen, not waiting. And waiting. And more waiting.

And when it came to the welfare of those she loved, her patience was in even shorter supply.

A strand of her hair caught, as it had several times already, on the collar of her shirt. She went to the bathroom, yanked a heavy-duty hair clip out of her bag of toiletries, gathered up the curly red mass and clipped it tightly to the back of her head.

A tiny uneven spot in the insole of her shoe made her yank it off and poke and dig at it until a fleck of something that looked like excess glue came off. She put the shoe back on and tested it.

That fixed, she then focused on the rough spot on the side of a fingernail that dragged annoyingly across everything she touched. Ten seconds with an emery board took care of that.

She cleaned her sunglasses. Grabbed a diet soda from the minibar, opened it, took a sip, and didn't want the rest. Tried some crackers, hated the taste. Brushed her teeth to get rid of it.

And through every movement, every busy-work item, she fought not to stare at the clock. And at her phone on the dresser, willing it to ring.

She knew she was losing her cool.

Some highly trained professional you are, she chastised herself.

But she knew this was different. Working cases was different, because she wasn't personally involved. Her life didn't hang in the balance, literally. So she was able to give her work the cool, dispassionate logic and intelligence required to do the best job possible.

But this was her grandfather, and all bets were off.

The longer it took, the more rationality fled and the more hideous the pictures her imagination painted became. If nothing was wrong, all Justin would need was one peek and a quiet spot to make the call. If he hadn't called yet, something must be wrong. Something awful had happened, G.C. was hurt or worse, and it was all her—

The ring of her cell made her leap for the dresser. Justin.

She flipped it open and breathlessly said hello.

"He's all right."

Weak-kneed with relief, she sank down on the end of the bed. Bless him for understanding that was what she needed to hear first. She wasn't sure what she said aloud, but it must have been some sort of thank-you, because of his response.

"You're welcome, honey. It would have been sooner, but they had some kind of group on a tour at Hoover, and it took twice as long as it should have to get out of there."

"That's fine," she said, still a bit giddy with relief. "As long as he's okay, nothing else matters."

"Alex," he said, then hesitated.

"What?"

"I should tell him."

"I don't want him to worry," she said.

"I don't want him to get caught off guard."

She hadn't thought of it that way. Her first instinct had been protection, but she hadn't really thought of the possibility that insulation wasn't the best way to accomplish that.

"He's as tough as he has to be, Alex," Justin said softly when she didn't respond. "But he should be warned, so he'll be on alert. He can handle it, but he has the right to know what he's up against."

She sighed. "You're right."

She knew it in her gut. That Justin had realized it when she hadn't added yet another layer to what was rapidly becoming a more complex situation than she'd ever faced in her personal life. Even her relationship with her mother, tangled and confused as it was, was easier. And her relationship with Emerson looked downright simple by comparison.

But then, it had been. They'd never delved beneath the surface much. And things would never, ever be like that with Justin. That was, she admitted now, part of what scared her, what held her off.

"I'll hang around until he's done," Justin said. "I'll have him call you, and then he and I can…discuss courses of action."

She felt a tug of anxiety. This was G.C.; she should be taking care of this; she should be there; she—

"Trust me, Alex. He matters to me, too. I'll take care of him."

His voice was low, soft, confident and supportive. As a declaration of his feelings for her, and his understanding of her feelings for her grandfather, it would be hard to top. She knew he was saying much more than his words, that he was letting her know that trusting him with the man she loved more than her own life would be an irrevocable step in the direction he wanted to go.

And suddenly she wanted it, too.

"I know you will," she said. "I'll wait for the call."

There was a pause during which she thought she heard him sigh. "Thank you," he finally said, and after they'd disconnected, she knew that the flood of revelations that had hit her had been exactly on the nose.

With the feeling of one who had just taken a huge

step, she set the phone down beside her. But she barely had time to absorb what had happened before a knock on the door had her on her feet again.

Instinctively she removed the Glock from its hidden holster in her bag and tucked it in the small of her back before she walked over to peer through the security lens in the door.

Lynn, still looking anxious, and with a large white envelope in her hand. Alex undid the dead bolt and the chain—she used the latter for the slow-down factor rather than in any hope it would ever stop someone determined to get in—and opened the door.

"This just came for you. Lieutenant Ryan asked that we hand deliver it. She didn't want to wait for you to get around to your e-mail."

"Thank you," Alex said as she took the envelope. That, she thought as the woman walked back toward the elevator, was one person who was going to be glad not to see her again.

She closed the door, secured it again, put the Glock back in its place, and only then opened the envelope. There was a note from Kayla on top, with the details of her chat with the maid. The woman had seen the man out in the hallway while she was working on the unexpectedly vacated room. When she'd returned to the cart for towels, he'd stopped, chatted her up for a moment, then asked for directions to the hotel's health club.

He had been perfectly nice, even affable, the maid

had said. Had even offered to tip her, although she said she had refused. She'd gone back to her cleaning, and he, she had thought, had gone on his way.

But Kayla had pressed, and the woman had finally admitted it was possible that after she'd gone back to work he had loitered a few minutes longer. It was routine practice to prop the room door open with the cart of cleaning supplies and towels, so while he couldn't have come in without her noticing, he could have had access to the door for a few minutes. Long enough to place something, tape most likely, over the door latch, so that it hadn't secured when the maid had finished and closed the door. Which would explain the slightly sticky residue Alex had found, and how he had gotten access to the room to position the newspaper.

The woman had felt bad enough to spend considerable time with their computer artist—although, Kayla added wryly in her note, the fact that the hotel was no doubt paying her for her time might have had something to do with it—and they'd come up with a good composite. Of course, Alex knew, any composite, even a good one, was only as good as the human memory providing the data.

But it was better than what she had now, which was nothing, she thought as she reached in for the image. It was a clue. It was a place to start.

She pulled out the composite.

She stared at the photo-like image, startled.

It wasn't the driver of the blue sedan. Not that she'd seen his face through the darkly tinted windows, but it didn't matter.

Because she had seen this man's. Twice.

It was the driver of the gardening truck.

Chapter 7

Someone was getting very nervous. And that told Alex one thing for sure—somebody was hiding something. Somebody had been hiding something ever since Marion had been murdered.

And unlike the casual-burglar suspect the police had originally created, that somebody still had something to lose.

Was it simply that they knew the statute of limitations never ran out on murder? Or was there more to it? Alex didn't want to become one of those who turned everything into a massive conspiracy, but after the recent revelations about Lab 33 and its connection to Athena, anything seemed possible.

She had called Kayla and let her know that the man the maid had seen outside her hotel room was the same man she'd seen on the road.

"He's good," she had told her friend. "He was ahead of me most of the time. And if it wasn't for this composite, I would never have known it was him. I zeroed in on another car that was acting suspiciously, seemed to be following me."

There was a momentary silence, and Alex could almost hear her old friend thinking, considering the possibilities.

"Any chance they were working together?" Kayla asked then.

The possibility had occurred to her. "Can't say they weren't," she said.

"Did you get a look at the license on the gardening truck?" Alex had already given her the plate info on the blue car that now seemed to be a dead end.

"No. It was covered up. I didn't think anything of it at the time, because it was just a burlap bag hanging down over the plate, the kind of thing you see in any truck like that."

"Any logo or name on the side?"

Alex closed her eyes and reformed the image in her mind, the dusty red truck festooned with rakes and mowers and blowers.

"No. Or if there was it was covered up."

"Driver only?"

"Yes."

"Where, and what was his DOT?"

Alex gave the direction of travel from the location she'd last seen the truck. It felt odd, to be on this side of giving a basic statement. She was the one usually asking the questions, even if it was only of the evidence brought to her.

"I can put this out to patrol," Kayla suggested. "See if we can find the guy."

Alex hesitated. "If he hasn't already figured it out, I'm not sure I want him to know just yet that he's been burned."

"And if he has realized it, he'll likely change his M.O."

"Yes," Alex agreed. "Dump the gardener's rig, at least. Although that was pretty clever."

"Very," Kayla agreed. "The kind of thing you look right past. So we're not dealing with some kind of rent-a-dope, hired just to trail you around."

"No."

Neither of the women needed to say anything more about the ramifications of that fact. Alex had known going in that she could be stirring up an Arizona scorpion's nest, but that didn't change the bottom line: the woman who had been the very heart and soul of Athena had been murdered, and now, for the first time in a decade, there might be a chance to find out who had done it and why. It was not a quest Alex would easily give up on.

* * *

The cell phone readout said "Unknown Name, Unknown Number," but Alex thought she recognized the voice that said tentatively, "Agent Forsythe?"

"Yes."

"This is Detective Hunt."

They'd already dispensed with last names in person, but he apparently felt the need for more formality on the phone. Or else he'd just wanted to be sure he had the right number. Or, perhaps, that she remembered him. Rather sweetly modest, she thought.

"Hi, Eric," she said cheerfully.

He sounded more relaxed after that. "I have that file you wanted. I wondered if you wanted to come by and see it, or if we could meet somewhere. I can bring it, as long as it doesn't leave my custody."

"That would be great. I'd like to talk to you about it anyway, get your feelings on some things." Then, guessing, she asked, "Looking for a reason to get out of the station?"

"Actually, yes," he answered, sounding a bit sheepish. "I have a new captain, and he's getting on my nerves."

"New-broom syndrome?"

He chuckled. "Something like that. He's got all kinds of new ideas, and he wants them all implemented."

"Immediately, of course."

"Of course."

"How about lunch somewhere?" she suggested.

"That would be great."

Rapport reestablished, Alex let him pick a place—somewhat removed from the station, she noticed—and they agreed to meet there in an hour. It was fifteen minutes away, so she spent the next forty-five continuing to go over his copious crime-scene and investigative notes from the murder. She wanted some clarification on a couple things.

When the room phone rang, she dropped everything and grabbed. Only G.C., Justin and a couple of the Cassandras knew where she was.

Well, and Lynn the manager, she thought wryly as she answered.

"Are we going to have a jurisdictional dispute over whose job it is to look after whom?"

Alex couldn't help laughing at her grandfather's officious tone. "Hi, G.C."

"Hello, my dear," he said, dropping back into his normal voice, although it held a note of sternness when he added, "I don't need you to protect me, you know."

"I know. Justin made that pretty clear."

"Good man, that. We had a nice long talk. Settled some things."

Alex's warning radar clamored suddenly. "Settled what things?" She couldn't help suspecting she'd been the topic of some of that settling.

"Some manly things," he said. "You will allow

that there are some things left in the world that are best kept between men?"

"As long as said men understand we leave them to you by choice, not necessity," Alex retorted. "And because they're probably too absurd for women to waste their time on."

G.C. laughed. "That's my ornery girl. Now, how are things progressing there?"

She hesitated for a moment before accepting the change of subject. The thought of Justin and her grandfather sitting down for a lengthy chat was unsettling to say the least. She couldn't help thinking she'd been one of the topics, no matter how she tried to tell herself she was being too self-important.

"I'm meeting with the detective who handled the case in about an hour. He's bringing the original file. Then I'll hit the court records, pull names of anybody who might have had a grudge against her as a prosecutor."

"Hmm," G.C. murmured. "She told me once of a case involving a brutal rape, where the defendant lunged at her in open court. The bailiffs had to restrain him, and he spent the rest of the trial shackled."

"Convicted?"

"Yes. When the verdict came in, he threatened her rather vociferously. Enough so that she mentioned it, although she refused any protection from the police. But that was her way."

"I remember," Alex said. In fact, if she'd had an

adult female role model in her life, one to combat the unwelcome teachings of her mother, it was probably Marion Gracelyn. "She was a very courageous woman."

"And stubborn," G.C. said, and again there was that undertone of affection in his voice. "The word *quit* just wasn't in her lexicon. Something I'm certain you can relate to."

"I can," Alex agreed sunnily, refusing to rise to the teasing bait. "And proud of it."

"As well you should be, my dear."

She was smiling when they hung up, once again thanking whatever fate had arranged for her to have such a wonderful man in her life.

She glanced at the clock, realized she needed to get moving. She restacked Eric's papers and fastened them back into the folder he'd neatly clipped them into, using a sticky note to mark her place so she could finish with them when she got back.

She wondered if he was as tidy at home as he was with his work. She'd known people whose organized ways stretched into all areas of their lives—such as her mother—but also just as many where it didn't. Some were methodical and detailed about their work and lived in disorder at home, and some the opposite, tidy at home but unable to work unless it was amid chaos.

She herself required a certain amount of order both places, but perfection was not on her priority list at home. She saved that for her lab work.

She realized with a little jolt that she didn't know what category Justin fell into. She knew he was fairly organized about his work, but when they met personally it was usually when he was visiting in D.C., and you couldn't judge such things from a hotel room. Or guest room, she added silently; they'd progressed to the point where he sometimes stayed at the farm when he was in town. He and G.C. got along famously, a fact strongly in his favor in Alex's book.

She reminded herself he was due back in Phoenix over the weekend, and felt the usual little thrill of anticipation she always seemed to feel at the thought of seeing him again. She'd never felt like this before, and she suddenly wondered if perhaps she should stop analyzing it all and simply enjoy.

"Enjoy," she muttered wryly as she gathered up the papers and her satchel. "What a concept."

Eric was already there when she arrived at the small coffee shop. He was, she noted, sitting in a booth at the back of the dining room, one which, by the nature of its location, was very secluded and would have minimal foot traffic passing by. The selection warned her he was wary about having the report out of the station, and she couldn't blame him.

"Thanks for bringing it," she said as she slid into the seat opposite him.

He gave a half shrug. "I figured the fewer people who knew I was even looking at it, the better."

"You've been through it again?"

He gave her a sideways look, as if trying to assess why she had asked. "Yeah. It still bothers me."

She liked him for that. She smiled at him, and he smiled back, although he seemed a bit embarrassed. She was saved from wondering why by the arrival of the waitress, who efficiently took her cheeseburger and a soda order and Eric's somewhat rueful request for a grilled chicken salad and iced tea and departed.

"Recoil," he explained, as if she'd asked. "My dad had to have a triple bypass a few months back, and he's only fifty-nine. Scared me."

"Scares me, too," she said. "I only eat like this on the road. At home I stay much closer to healthy eating, with only the occasional foray into decadence and indulgence."

That won her a grin. "That's my theory. The occasional foray is necessary."

He slid the thick file across the table to her. She opened it and began to read and take notes, forcing herself to forget that the blunt, grim descriptions were referring to a woman she'd known and liked. It brought back memories of having to do the same with reports about Rainy's death. This was one area in which practice definitely did not make things easier. Sometimes the pain was as fresh and sharp as if it had been only yesterday.

She continued while they ate—after stealthily concealing the file while the waitress delivered their plates—knowing the detective would understand. He busied himself working on something else, tapping data into his PDA. And later playing a game of some kind; she caught a glimpse of a colored ball flying across the screen and blowing up several others.

When her cell rang, Alex almost let it go to voice mail until she saw who it was: Allison, at last returning her call. After perfunctory niceties, Allison quickly picked up that something serious was going on. Alex gave her the digest version, telling Marion's daughter she was with the detective who had investigated the case right now.

"My God. You think you're really onto something about my mother's murder?"

"It's possible. It may go nowhere, but…"

"You don't think so."

"My gut doesn't."

"Good," Allison said bluntly. "I never believed that garbage about her interrupting a burglary," she said, echoing Alex's own thoughts. "I wish I could fly out there right now."

"I know." Alex didn't even want to speculate on what Allison was tied up with. "If there's more, if there's finally an answer, I'll find it," she told her sister.

"I know you will." Allison's tone had been one of absolute certainty, and Alex wasn't about to let her down. "Contact me when you can give me the whole story."

"I will."

It took her most of the meal to slog through the main portion of the numerous reports in the file. Murder cases were never, ever simple or short. That of a senator was beyond voluminous.

Photos and diagrams added more pages, so it was a while before she got to the supplemental reports. These she wanted to read carefully, because it was there that any theories that came to the investigators, suspicions, possibilities, all the things they couldn't substantiate with empirical evidence, were laid out.

When the table had been cleared and refills on their drinks provided, she leaned back in the vinyl-upholstered booth and looked across the table at him.

"Was there anything that particularly stuck in your gut?"

"Yes," he said, quickly enough that she knew he'd been thinking about it recently. "This. It was listed 'Not for Press Release' on the public copy, so the page isn't in the report, but I had one."

She looked at the paper he slid toward her, at the spot he indicated with one finger—he chewed his nails, she noticed, a not unusual habit for people in stressful jobs. But then her attention was seized by what was on the page he had indicated.

It was a copy of a summary of bank statements, pulled after Marion's death. And beginning months before her murder was a series of regular, weekly cash withdrawals of five thousand dollars.

"We couldn't find where it was going, or why it had started, after," he said. "Rich lady like that, our first thought was drugs, but the autopsy tox screen didn't show any sign."

Alex managed to stifle her reaction to the very thought of Marion Gracelyn using drugs. "That would have been a pretty big jump, from nothing to a five-thousand-a-week habit," she said neutrally.

"That's what I thought," he agreed. "And from what I knew of her, she wasn't the type. I didn't know her personally, of course, but I knew of her, and it just didn't fit."

"No, it didn't. Still doesn't."

He nodded. "But I was junior at the time. I got to spend all my time saying 'no comment' to the gazillion reporters who kept hanging around, making things up when we wouldn't talk to them. Vultures."

"I know the feeling," she said; she'd had her own run-ins with the media. "But you were right," Alex continued. "She wasn't the type. At all."

He nodded, his satisfaction at being vindicated no doubt muted by how much time had passed. And that his then-partner wasn't around to hear it.

"Any other ideas that hit you back then, about that money?"

"Other than she just went on several regular shopping binges?"

Now shop was something Marion could do, Alex thought. Her children, David and Allison—another

Athenian—had rarely lacked for anything. And Marion herself had always dressed with an exquisite sense of style and flair. But she hadn't been profligate.

"Other than legitimate, if extravagant, expenditures, yes," she said.

He looked at her, hesitated, then finally said, "Blackmail."

Alex blinked. She couldn't imagine Marion ever doing anything that she could be blackmailed over, but she had to admit the mechanics of it fit—the sudden commencement of the withdrawals, a set amount, cash only, all those factors supported the idea. They fit other scenarios, as well, but she couldn't deny this possibility, not with those indicators.

"But," Eric added, "we couldn't find anything else to indicate that was what was happening. No phone calls from unknown numbers, no late-night excursions to deliver money, nothing."

"So that idea didn't fly."

"No. But we never did find out what the real reason was."

"Which is why it bugs you to this day," Alex speculated.

Eric's mouth curled up wryly. "I don't like loose ends."

"Neither do I," Alex said, and made a mental note to pass on this bit of discovery to Allison the next time she spoke to her. If her mother had been being blackmailed, she'd want to know.

If she didn't know already, Alex thought. Not much got by Allison. Ever.

Alex knew she needed to tread carefully on this next topic. "Did anyone, after the murder, go back to the previous incidents Marion reported?"

"You mean the fire, and the thing with her car?"

She supposed the fact that he knew what she meant answered her question. "Yes."

"I did. Fire was arson, but there was a string of them in that neighborhood that summer. No reason to think hers was targeted."

"Nothing different about it?"

"Other than it was her house, no. Same M.O., same accelerant, even the same location on the house."

"Were there any more after hers?"

He blinked. Thought. "No," he finally said. "Not that I remember. They just…stopped."

Because she'd been the intended target all along, the others just camouflage? Alex wondered.

She saw by the look on his face that he was thinking the same thing.

"What about the car?" she asked.

"Nothing that could prove intent," he said. "The lines were intact. Reservoir was at the right level. There were no unaccounted-for prints on the car or the power-steering fluid cap. Nothing to indicate someone put anything in or tampered with the system."

"So if someone did—" she began.

"They were very, very good," he finished.

So he was taking this seriously, she thought. Enough to admit the possibilities that might have been missed.

"How would you do it, if you didn't want to get caught?" she asked him.

He thought for a moment. "Maybe inject the contaminant with a syringe, into the reservoir. You wouldn't even have to touch anything, could do it above the fill line, so that it would never leak and get noticed. And a tiny needle hole near the cap could easily get overlooked or written off as normal wear or a defect."

She nodded. "That makes sense."

"They didn't want to listen to me about those things, either," Eric said. "Thought I was talking like some conspiracy whack-nut."

"When this is over," Alex said, "I'll make sure that they all know they should have listened."

He smiled at that. Then, after a moment he asked, "So, if this isn't an official inquiry, are you on vacation?"

"I'm on my own time, yes."

Not taking any time off for years was finally paying off, she thought. She had a ton of time on the books, and it had come in handy during the investigation of Rainy's case, and it was beginning to look as if that pattern would repeat now. Cold cases, she was quickly learning, did not come together quickly.

"Boyfriend doesn't mind?"

"He's FBI, too," she said, although it still seemed odd to her to refer to Justin that way. Not, however, as odd as it once had. Was she getting used to it? Or simply more convinced it was true? "He understands."

"Oh."

He looked oddly deflated, and only then did Alex realize that he might have been asking in the hopes of learning whether she was involved or not. And only then did she realize her response had felt utterly natural. So on some level her mind was already moving ahead in that arena.

"Figures," Eric said with a good-natured show of exaggerated glumness. "Not only is there a boyfriend, but he's armed."

She laughed. "Why, that's the sweetest thing I've heard all day."

"Your day better improve, then," he joked.

"I can't believe some lucky girl doesn't have you all wrapped up," she said, meaning it.

"Not likely." The glumness was a bit more real this time.

"Why not? You're cute, funny, charming and a darn good cop."

She'd succeeded in thoroughly embarrassing him

this time. He stumbled for a moment, then seized on what she guessed felt safest.

"How do you know I'm a good cop?"

"I've read through all your notes," she reminded him. "If that's how thorough and perceptive you were back then with no experience, you've probably only gotten better since."

He was red-faced now. "Geez. You need another favor or what?"

She laughed and cut him some slack. "Oh, probably, eventually. But it's still true."

"Thanks." Clearly still embarrassed, he quickly changed the subject, gesturing at the file she'd now closed. "So, what do you think?"

"I'm still processing it all," she said truthfully. "There's a lot there, as you know better than anyone. So let me ask you something. Since you've had all this percolating in the back of your mind for years, now…what's your best theory?"

"Not a burglar," he said. "There was more to it than that."

Gratified to hear him echo her own feelings, she prompted him to go on. "What makes you think so?"

"The attack was too…organized. Methodical. She didn't stumble on somebody who reacted out of fear or desperation to get away."

"You think it was planned?"

He hesitated, then said, "I think—and I don't have

a damn thing to prove it—that he was waiting for her. Not just anyone. Her."

Alex let out a breath she hadn't even been aware of holding. So he'd seen what she'd seen. He hadn't even had the benefit of Marion's letter and he'd seen it.

"I agree," she said softly.

Chapter 8

The lying-in-wait theory had taken up residence in Alex's mind with her first look at the diagram and photos of the crime scene. She knew that room at Athena so well, she knew exactly where Marion had been when she'd been struck down. And her three-dimensional knowledge made it easy for her to picture the sequence of the attack.

A nighttime intruder could have easily hidden in the shadow of the big storage cabinets that stood around the perimeter of the entire room and never been noticed by someone who had no idea there was a problem. The unsuspecting Marion most likely would have walked right by without seeing a thing.

Which, of course, had given him a tremendous advantage—the opportunity to catch her completely by surprise. The fact that he'd attacked her when he could have safely stayed hidden told Alex this hadn't been coincidence, or just a matter of Marion being in the wrong place at the wrong time. That had been a thin theory before, but with what she now knew, it had even more holes in it.

Enough holes to make it totally implausible.

She wondered why the police had given up so easily. Eric had told her that, as the junior officer, he'd had little input, had even been scoffed at when he tried—but why had his superiors let it go so easily? Had it simply been eagerness to put this high-profile, pressure-laden case behind them? Or was there more to it? Pressure from outside, perhaps?

Several nefarious and repugnant possibilities came to mind, and she didn't like the smell of any of them. She didn't like believing the world could really run that way, but she knew it could.

As she drove toward the county administration building, which housed the main office of the county attorney, she pondered the growing mountain of questions. She knew that one of the most basic tenets of law enforcement was that in most cases, the simplest, most obvious answer was the true one.

But in this case, she just couldn't believe it.

It would, she thought as she made the turn onto

Jefferson and began to look for parking, be so much easier to just take the path of least resistance.

But Athenas never took the easy road.

She stuffed a bottle of water into her satchel—and removed her weapon and locked it in the trunk, since taking it into the building would be more hassle than it was worth—and headed for the doors. There weren't that many people left who had been there when Marion had been the county attorney, so she guessed talking to them wasn't going to take too much time.

It was what she had to do after this that was going to eat up the hours.

When she left the building three hours later, the only thing she knew for sure was that if anyone had anything bad to say about Marion Gracelyn, they were keeping it to themselves.

She'd run into situations before where death suddenly elevated an ordinary person to near sainthood. It was a normal response born of complex human emotions, and she'd been trained to look beyond it for the truth. But those cases had been for the most part without the complication of legal and political machinations.

Unlike this one. No one got to the rank of U.S. senator without making an enemy or two along the way, but if Marion's were in the county attorney's office, they were deeply hidden now.

She went back to the hotel with a handful of notes, stopping for ice at the vending area on her floor.

Once she was at her room she carefully inspected the several markers she'd left in place after the maid had finished cleaning.

The thin thread she fastened at the top of the door, where no one would likely look, remained unbroken and attached. The faint dusting of powder she'd spread inside the door was undisturbed, no sign of a footprint. The bit of tape she'd left on the inside lip of the drawer that contained her laptop was intact, the thread tied to the inner latch of her suitcase unbroken.

Everything else was as she'd left it; the book on the nightstand at the same exact angle, the drapes open exactly the length of her forearm, the bathroom door exactly the length of her running shoe away from the edge of the tub.

She was as certain as she could be that no one had been in the room. Or if they had, they were so good she wouldn't have been able to tell anyway.

She got out her laptop, connecting the power cord for what she knew was going to be a marathon session. As it booted up, she quickly changed into some casual yoga pants and a T-shirt, put some ice in a glass and filled it with water, then sat down at the table to begin.

First, she turned off her cell phone; just about everyone she knew had the number, and she didn't want to be interrupted for casual chat. She'd given only the people she would want to talk to right now the hotel name and number, trusting even the hotel-routed landline more than the too-easily monitored cell phone just now.

She logged on to the FBI system, went through the security process and started. The list of names, all of them culled from cases Marion had prosecuted, was long and varied. It took her a few minutes to get into the rhythm of the system; she was much more familiar with the evidence software than running suspects.

The first one she checked was the rapist G.C. had mentioned. Gary Finkle. The man had gotten out of prison, briefly, but he'd immediately gone back to his old ways and was back inside in less than a year, this time with no possibility for parole, after he'd murdered his next victim.

"So much for rehabbing sexual predators," Alex muttered and went on.

She wished things were as simple as they seemed on television; she'd love to be able to wrap this up in an hour or so of fast-paced effort.

Maybe with music, she thought. A nice rock score.

Laughing inwardly at her silliness, Alex plowed on, knowing that if nothing promising turned up among these names, she was going to have to start digging through Marion's senatorial records, to see if there was anyone she'd somehow mortally offended there.

She worked through the late afternoon, only stopping to order a sandwich she could eat on the side when the protesting growls of her empty stomach became annoyingly distracting.

After it arrived she settled back in the chair and began again, pausing for bites of food now and then. In between names, while awaiting results that would tell her whether to add that person to the possibles list—if they'd been in jail and were still in jail it was easier—she continued to go through Eric's personal notes on the murder case.

She smiled at one entry that read, "Ayers says Gracelyn was hell on wheels. From his tone, I think she must have run over him in court once or twice."

The computer beeped. Alex looked up to see the dialog box indicating another search completed. This one was still in prison at Yuma, so she put him on the "unlikely" list. She input the next name, took a bite of her meat loaf sandwich, then went back to the notes.

She turned the next page. A big "?" scrawled on the back caught her eye.

The replica of the spider web he'd drawn below it caught her breath.

She scanned the rest of the notes quickly, but saw no mention or explanation of the image. She glanced at her watch, decided it wasn't too late, got up and went to her satchel to dig out Eric's phone number. She picked up the room phone and dialed.

He answered on the second ring.

"Yeah, I remember that spider thing," he said when she asked about the drawing. "It kept popping up on papers and stuff of hers we were going through. I could never tie it to anything, though."

"No pattern to what you found it on?"

"Nope. If I remember right, it was on the corner of a newspaper or magazine or something, then on a bank statement, and on the back of a bill of some kind where there were other notes."

Alex stifled a sigh. If she only knew if it was connected, she could either pursue it or not waste the time. Not that she had the slightest idea how to ferret out the meaning of the cryptic symbol Marion had repeated so often.

"Anything I can do to help?" Eric offered.

She almost asked how fast he could type names in a form, but held back.

"If I think of anything else, I'll let you know. Thanks, Eric."

She'd barely replaced the receiver when the phone beneath her hand rang. Considering who knew she was here, she picked it up quickly, hoping it might be G.C.

"Hello?"

"Your line was busy."

The male voice was instantly familiar, but the words got her back up almost as quickly.

"I was working, Justin."

There was a pause before he said mildly, "It wasn't an accusation. Just letting you know in case it wasn't you on the phone, all things considered."

"Oh." She felt more than a little sheepish. "Sorry."

"That's not me, Alex. I'll never try to own you."

Sometimes he was downright disconcerting with

his razor-sharp perceptiveness. She didn't know what to say to that, so, perhaps wisely, she kept silent.

"You sound harried. Overloaded?"

"A bit. But I knew this was going to be a big undertaking. Marion affected a lot of people during her career. I've only tackled the ones as prosecutor and I've got over thirty names."

"Want me to check the senatorial records while I'm still here?"

The offer was beyond tempting; it would really give her a leg up, because even if something turned up in this batch of names, she couldn't be sure that was the final answer. Angry suspects threatened a lot, but actually carried out the threats much less often.

"It would be a big job," she said, hedging a little.

"I figured that. But I'm here now. And although I'd much rather be there, with you, I'm guessing that the sooner you have your answers, the better for the man who wants you all to himself for a while."

There wasn't a change in his voice, it didn't slip into that husky register that made her toes curl, but there was something about the pure and simple intensity of them that told her things were about to change. Or maybe it was just that her own outlook had changed, and she was hearing him through that filter now.

Whichever it was, she had a feeling it didn't matter. The result was going to be the same.

"Yes," she said. "I'd like you to do that."

She heard him take in a quick breath, and knew he hadn't missed the message beneath the words.

"I'll be in touch," he said, and hung up so quickly it left her a little breathless.

Or perhaps it was the thought of what she'd just done.

She needed air.

And space.

And no people.

She picked up the phone and made another call. Spoke briefly to Christine, who laughed and gave her the okay for her plan.

Only hard-won discipline made her slow herself down and do things methodically. She shut down, packed up and secured her laptop, locked all the paperwork in the room safe and double-checked the balcony slider. Then she quickly changed into jeans and a lightweight, long-sleeved shirt and the boots she'd brought for just this purpose. She grabbed her bag, made sure there was a full water bottle in it, and lastly set up her usual intruder-warning signs.

And then she was out and on her way. Heading for a place where she could always clear her head. The place that had made her what she was, who she was.

She was going home to Athena.

Charm nickered a greeting.

Alex was always surprised when the mare actually remembered her, she saw her so infrequently. But then again, the gray was her own beloved Lacy's granddaughter, and anything was possible. Regardless, the greeting was definite and welcoming, as was the nudging of her shoulder when she stopped rubbing under the jaw too soon for the mare's taste.

"I know you've had a busy week, m'girl, teaching all those new riders a thing or four. But how about a ramble up in the hills with me?"

The horse butted her arm emphatically.

"I'll take that as a yes," she said with a laugh.

With the speed and skill of a lifetime of practice, she had the gray groomed, tacked up and ready to go. She borrowed a ball cap—the one thing she'd forgotten—from the tack room, pulled her hair into a ponytail through the gap in the back and settled it to shade her face. She led the eager mare out into the early-evening light and swung up into the saddle.

The moment she cleared the school grounds Alex felt the odd mood begin to lift. There had been few problems in her life that had been helped by a long ride on a good horse. Not only was it a passion in and of itself, but it helped her think, and that was something she needed to do a lot of right now. Not to mention the interesting things that had happened, she thought with a smile, remembering the last time she'd ridden this trail. Justin had been watching her then, and her life had been about to change, though she hadn't known it. Yet.

She had a lot of data on Marion and her life. And

her death. The problem came in trying to tie it all together in a way that made sense. A way that could steer her in the right direction. A way that could bring justice, albeit belatedly, to the visionary who had made this place possible.

As she rode, the ground began to rise beneath them. Clearing the first hill above the school had always been a marker for her. Once you started down the other side, and the sprawl of Athena was out of sight, you could easily imagine there was no one and nothing for miles around. The landscape was un-tamed and unmarred, much as it had been before man of any persuasion had set foot here. It was starkly beautiful, and contrary to what many thought, full of life.

And utterly, totally unforgiving.

It was also one of Athena's best training tools. One of the first things newcomers were taught was that it could kill. The desert didn't care if you were weak or hurt or thirsty or lost. It is what it is, they were told, and no amount of talking, bargaining or whining would ever change it.

Either you learned how to survive, and then thrive, or you didn't and the desert won. Those who made it through learned that there wasn't much difference between that impassive desert and life. Expecting it to change because you weren't up to the battle was like playing Russian roulette with an automatic.

They were halfway down the other side of the

first rise when Charm—short for Charmeuse, one of the textiles on which the Forsythe family fortune had been built—suddenly shied.

Alex collected the mare, drawing in the reins with the featherlight touch that was all that was necessary with this horse. Still the gray snorted and tossed her head in protest. Or in warning...

Alex was jolted back to her situation. She'd thought herself safe here, but then, she'd thought that before. Evil had struck at Athena more than once, and there was nothing that said it couldn't happen again. And wasn't she investigating one of the worst incidences of it? And if she'd been followed to her hotel, as it seemed she had, why not here?

Charm snorted again and danced sideways, away from a clump of sage growing over a boulder. The horse pivoted on her forelegs, keeping her eye warily on the brush. Then she shook her head at it. The actions were familiar, and Alex adjusted her assessment. Judging by the air temperature and the time of year, she guessed snake.

"Good girl," she soothed the horse, and guided her carefully out of range. That it was a rattler seeking out the warmth of the sun-heated rock was not a theory she cared to prove. She was fortunate to be on a sensitive, clever animal, and glad not to be so stupid she thought she knew more than the horse's finely tuned senses.

They went on, Charm forging forward willingly,

Alex sucking in long, deep breaths of the clean desert air that was not yet too hot. The messages were both strong and faint, the tang of the creosote brush, the radiation of the sun that promised the blistering heat of the summer to come. All of it was familiar and loved, and she—

Charm leaped as a smaller boulder in front of them oddly cracked.

A sound echoed. Twanged. An all-too-familiar sound.

A ricochet.

Someone was shooting at them.

Chapter 9

Alex hadn't seen what direction the shot had come from. And the ricochet had distorted the direction of the sound. She was certain she hadn't heard the shot itself. Silenced? Possible.

She made a split-second judgment based on the crack in the stone the fired round had hit. The shooter was likely above them.

She spun Charm on her haunches and put her heels to the gray's flanks. A puff of dirt spattered as another round struck near the horse's heels—too near. The mare bounded forward, taking the twisting, rock-strewn slope as if it were a grassy pasture back at the farm. The nimble horse responded to Alex's slightest cue and never put a foot wrong on the treacherous ground.

Within seconds they were down in a gully that Alex hoped would make further shots impossible for the moment. Assuming that she was right about where the shooter had been, the angle should protect them.

She nudged Charm up against the steep side of the gully. The horse was clearly unsettled but went as asked. Alex slowly, and as quietly as possible, walked the horse south, to where she knew the bank had been undercut by a flash flood years ago.

She found the spot she'd remembered, a bit bigger now, perhaps enlarged by subsequent storms. Charm wasn't happy about the low overhang, but she was well trained and went in under it, anyway. A good partner, Alex thought, like when we turned the tables on Justin.

She waited, listening, calming the horse with a soothing touch when she got restless enough to move around. Charm quickly got the idea they were staying put a while and settled down. Alex crouched beside her, closing her eyes for a moment to focus on her most useful sense at the moment, hearing.

Slowing her own breathing to a shallow minimum, Alex strained to listen for any movement that sounded out of place. Nothing.

Then came the familiar squawk of a cactus wren, a sound she knew as well as the whinny of a horse. But her breath stopped when the naturally skittish bird began a chatter that sounded much like a dog warning an invader off his turf.

An invader…

With a mental thanks to the bird for the warning, she stood up. Charm's head came up.

"I need a favor, sweetheart," she whispered, and the horse's alert ears flicked forward.

Alex reached into the saddlebag where she'd deposited her backup bottle of water. She opened it, turned toward the horse and poured a small amount over the pommel of the saddle and let it run down the seat. She rubbed it in, knowing she'd have to oil the leather up later.

When she was done, she stepped back slightly. The darkened spot on the tanned leather stood out even here in the shade. From a distance, to someone expecting it, it could easily be mistaken for blood.

She took the rest of her supplies out of the bags. They were fairly minimal since she'd only planned on an afternoon's ride, but more than a novice would have brought, since she well knew the precariousness of life in the desert. She checked her cell phone; she was getting a signal, if only a couple bars. But the hunter was too close now, if she used the phone the sound of her voice would lead him right to her. As would the ring, she realized, and turned it off before she shoved it into a back pocket.

Then she tossed the reins back over the horse's head, turned her to the opening and shooed her out.

"Home, Charm. Go home," she whispered.

The horse hesitated for a moment. It was something they were trained for, but these circumstances were unusual. Alex risked a slight rise in the volume of her whispered urging.

"Get, girl. Home."

The gray flicked her ears once more, then trotted off, back the way they had come. Alex watched until the horse clambered up the bank and went out of sight. She clipped the Glock in its holster at the small of her back. She pulled on the gloves that had been in the bags. Then she took out the knife that she always sheathed in her boot when in the desert.

With great care, and not without some damage, she went to work with the knife just outside the overhang. She cut away at the local plant life, moving as quickly as she could, but still listening every second for any warning sounds. She heard the scrape of something on stone before she was satisfied with her efforts, but she had little choice but to take cover now.

She ducked back under the overhang and waited. She ignored the stinging of her hands where the sharp spines had stabbed her.

With any luck, her hunter had seen that dark spot on the saddle and thought he'd gotten her, thought that she was down and helpless, and all he had to do was come ahead and verify she was dead or finish her off.

Come on down, she thought, her body gearing up, muscles taut, nerves tingling and aware, brain ready.

She thought she heard a faint muttering from above, about where she and Charm had come down the lesser slope, and near where Charm had gone back riderless. When the sound became clearer, closer, she smiled. A cool, merciless smile. Taking a shot at her was one thing, it came with the territory. Endangering her horse was another thing altogether. And he'd pay for that.

She pressed herself up against the side of the overhang. She heard a small tumble of sound, pebbles and sliding sand. Just what she'd expected to hear. Then a heavier sound. A thud. The voice again, louder.

"Shit!"

Male. Pissed. Clumsy? The possibilities ran through her mind rapidly.

More pebbles rattling. Another thud.

"I know I hit her. The bitch has got to be dead, damn it, that should be good enough."

Hope you believe in ghosts, Alex thought.

And on another level she was wondering, Good enough for who?

That this wasn't the man himself who was after her, but someone working for him, was added to the various plans she was making. It could make a difference. Mainly in just how much he was willing to risk to get her.

The man apparently gave up on stealth. His progress now was clearly audible. And then he ran into her handiwork and his presence was trumpeted.

"Damn! Son of a bitch!"

The string of curses went on, accompanied by the sound of scrambling feet in sand. Alex ignored the impressive vocabulary. This was her chance. She darted out from the overhang.

He was dancing. Dancing amid the piles of stabbing cholla cactus, famous for its habit of seemingly jumping at unwary passersby, that she'd left for him to blunder into.

He hopped, brushing madly at his legs, then yanking back his hands. Continuing to swear.

But most important, looking anywhere but at her.

She was on him before he even realized she was there. He went down hard, facedown, yelling. She dug a knee into his back. He squirmed, trying to throw her off, but she had the leverage. And the knife.

Quickly she searched him for weapons. She found a small automatic, but a sniff at it told her it hadn't been fired. She'd figured he'd been using a rifle of some kind; he didn't seem the type to want to get any closer than he had to, not to a target that might shoot back.

She pocketed the small gun, wondering in passing what crimes she might be able to link it to back in the lab. But that was for later.

She found a small cell phone, with the logo of one of the pay-as-you-go companies. That could yield some interesting information, she thought, and shoved it in her pocket, as well.

Then she grabbed a handful of mousy-brown hair.

Yanked his head back. Slowly she moved her knife past the man's eyes, tilting it so it glinted in the desert sun on its way to his exposed throat.

"Son of a bitch," he repeated.

"Daughter, actually. Although I'm sure mumsy wouldn't care for the expression, I won't argue with you. You want to say anything else while you still have vocal cords?" she asked, making her tone purposely breezy.

He clearly was afraid to move too much with that blade against his jugular. "Fuck you."

"Well, that's helpful. Okay, then."

She tightened her grip on his hair and pulled his head back farther, digging her knee harder into his kidneys. She shifted the hilt of the knife in her hand, as if to get a better grip before slicing his throat.

He yelped. "Hey! No, wait!"

"Why?" She knew she sounded only vaguely curious.

"Because…" He gulped, she could feel the strain of his muscles as she held him in the uncomfortable position. "You can't just kill me."

"Why not? You were going to kill me, after all. I mean, I could just leave you for the desert to kill, but where's the fun in that?"

"Son of a bitch," he said again, apparently in a rut at the moment. "What kind of woman are you?"

She gave his head a yank. And for the first time, she let some of the fury she was feeling into her voice. "I'm an Athena," she hissed. "The kind of woman punks like you don't want to admit exists. The kind of woman who makes you look like the cowardly, pathetic, impotent vermin you are."

He was angry enough to risk the blade and gave a furious jerk. The movement made her nick his throat. He twisted to get away. She let him, for an instant, just enough for him to roll over onto his back so she could see his face, read his eyes. And confirm what she'd already seen: whoever he was, he wasn't the gardener. Which meant she could make no assumptions about how many people were involved in this.

She saw him think he had her, that he could get free, for a split second before she brought her knee down again, this time hard into his gut. Air whistled out of him and he gasped. She settled the knife against his throat again, schooling her expression to dispassionate coolness.

"I'm also," she added, her voice even again, "the woman who knows this desert well enough to make sure you're never found. Someday decades from now a flash flood may wash your bones down to the highway, but until then, nobody will know. And by then, nobody will care. Assuming anybody cares now, of course."

She moved again, letting him breathe as she settled the knife in her palm, making him yelp anew. "Don't you want to know who sent me?"

She'd already decided how to play this. She laughed. "Do you really think I don't already know?"

Confusion flickered across his face. "You do? He said you wouldn't. That you couldn't know."

"He underestimated. Just like he overestimated you."

"But…he said you were FBI. That if anything went wrong you'd just arrest me."

So, he knew who and what she was. And was willing to risk the murder of a federal agent. He must be getting paid a lot.

While she still didn't know who was footing the bill, she did know something about him now: he had lousy taste in henchmen. And this attempt on her life spoke volumes about the size and value of the secret he was so desperate to keep.

"I'm off duty," she said. "And nobody's ever going to know."

"He'll guess," the man insisted. "I'm supposed to call him when it's over. He gave me that phone you took, so he could call for a report. He'll get suspicious if I don't answer."

"Don't worry about it," she said, in the tone of a parent soothing a worried child. "I'll answer for you and let him know you failed. Completely."

The man twisted, his face contorting in anger. She ignored him.

"Hmm," she murmured, making her voice studiedly casual, as if she were thinking something over.

"Maybe I should let you live, and let him take care of you for me. Shouldn't take him too long to find somebody else who's more…efficient."

The man swore as his face reddened. She could see he'd had a bellyful of her insults, but still didn't have the nerve to go up against that knife. There was something up close and personal about a blade as a weapon, and for cowards it was one of the most intimidating, if for no other reason than it told you the person you were up against wasn't afraid to do just that—get up close and personal.

And nothing scared a coward more than a lack of fear in someone else. They didn't teach human psychology at Athena for nothing.

"Where did he find you, anyway?" She took a chance with a guess. "He's not the type to hang out where your kind does."

He gave her a look that was filled with nothing less than hatred. But he answered. "His kid is."

"Ah. I'd heard rumors," she said, trying to lead him on, to get anything she could out of him that might provide another piece to the puzzle. "But you know, people talk, it might not be true."

The man snorted. "Kid's a coke-head who fried his brain years ago."

Well, that adds another layer, she thought. I wonder whose kid? The gardener's, maybe?

"And how good it must make Dad feel, to know somebody like you feels superior to his doper kid."

"He don't care. He only worries about what his boss thinks. And wants."

"Like me dead?" she suggested, and saw the answer in his eyes.

So. Whoever had hired this piece of work—the gardener or maybe somebody else—had also been hired by somebody else, Alex mused. The head of the food chain? Or just another link? Just how long was this thread that led back to the person who didn't want her digging into Marion's murder? How much distance had he put between himself and the attempts to stop her?

As much as he could, she thought. It only made sense. She'd already deduced whoever it was had a lot to lose. Or gain, if the motive had been as simple as vengeance. Problem was, what was of value to one person could be completely disregarded by the next, so unless you knew what was important to that person, you didn't really know where to look.

"Maybe," she said thoughtfully, "you just might have something to bargain with after all."

The man had gone pale. Probably because as she'd spoken, she'd idly tapped the knife blade against this throat. She smiled at him. He didn't look encouraged.

"Unless, of course, he paid you enough to die for him," she said.

Chapter 10

"What did you find at the scene besides the weapon?" Kayla asked.

Alex settled the headset earpiece more firmly in her ear so she could continue sorting the papers she'd jammed rather haphazardly in the hotel room safe as she talked to her friend.

In true Athena fashion, Kayla had leaped into action when Alex called from the desert. A marked police unit had arrived in less than twenty minutes to take charge of her assailant, leaving Alex free to process the scene. It didn't take her long to locate the rifle he'd used, with the makeshift silencer. A quick inspection told her how lucky she was. If he'd bothered to maintain his weapon, or secured one in better shape, she might well be dead right now.

"Shell casings. Right amount for the number of shots. Tracks, one good enough for a shoe print. Your CSI's doing that. Oh, and I had her bag a couple of cholla needles. Looks like they have the suspect's blood on them." She could have turned over her knife, as well, for it's tiny droplet, but decided it might be wise to keep that to herself. "May not need DNA, but you never know."

"And you can never have too much evidence," Kayla agreed.

Kayla had offered to come out to Athena herself, but Alex had declined. Her friend was much more experienced at interrogating than she herself was, so she had asked that she take care of that, to see if she could get any more information out of this desert rat.

"Anything more from him?"

"I didn't have much more luck," Kayla said. "He told me the same thing he told you. Insisted he'd never met the guy who hired the guy who hired him. He was paid in cash left at a drop, half now, the second half to be delivered when he provided proof you were dead."

In any woman except one from Athena, Alex might have expected a bit more emotion, worry or panic in the voice. But Kayla was Athenian through and through, and spoke as calmly as Alex had.

"Where was the drop?" Alex asked.

"The library, if you can believe it."

"Ours? The one in Athens, I mean?"

"Yes. I checked with Mr. Lang."

The now-forty-something man—he'd been in his twenties when they'd first seen him, and drop-dead gorgeous—was the antithesis of the librarian stereotype. He loved football, climbed mountains, ran marathons and laughed aloud more than any man Alex had ever known. When he'd taken charge, he'd even set aside a separate room in the library for people to violate the no talking—or laughing—rule.

Tongues had wagged at first, but it worked, and the main room of the building was blissfully quiet for those who needed it. And the laughing room, as they called it, had become a cool haven for kids who, without it, might be up to who knows what mischief out on the streets.

And, Mr. Lang pointed out, if they were around books enough, they seemed to absorb their importance, and that was half his job done. And to this day, even though he was only a decade or so older than they were, they called him Mr. Lang.

"He remembered the guy?" Alex asked.

"He did. You know how he is, he knows everybody who comes in, practically. So he noticed this guy as a newcomer."

"Did he come in more than once?"

"Off and on for a couple of weeks. Mostly on the computer stations."

"E-mailing his boss," Alex guessed.

"That was my thought, too."

"Mr. Lang said the records, cookies, et cetera are all cleared once a patron's session is over. So are check-out records, once the item is returned, unless there was a fine or a hold involved."

"Standard response," Alex sighed. "I don't want to have to lean on Mr. Lang."

"I didn't think you would, any more than I would. I asked him to tell us as much as he was comfortable with."

"And?"

"Your guy used a Phoenix library card number to reserve a computer station for a specific date and time."

Alex blinked. "An assassin with a library card?"

"With somebody's," Kayla said. "That reservation buys him up to an hour, but he only used about ten minutes of it."

Alex's mind was racing. "Do you think Mr. Lang would give us records on any cards that have been reported stolen or missing?"

"He will. They're on the way. He reasoned that since they were already out of the possession of the rightful owner, and thus couldn't reflect on them, they were fair game."

Alex smiled, widely. "Woman, you are a wonder."

"Just a good cop."

"More than that, my friend. Much more."

As she hung up, Alex wondered if the happiness at having Kayla back in her life would ever abate.

The estrangement between them had been long and unpleasant for two who had been like sisters, so she doubted if she would ever take the relationship for granted again. Kayla was long past her lousy taste in men, and Alex wasn't about to judge anyone on that subject ever again.

She went back to the papers spread out across the table. She'd begun a grid on her laptop, several columns of items that went from solid evidence and theories to things that seemed odd, important for reasons she couldn't explain or unexpected and thus worthy of attention. Things that hadn't been connected to anything but were little blips on the radar of normalcy went into the grid: personal observations, likely candidates for murderer and the sources of all of the information.

Those who were connected she put in different text colors, until she had twisting threads of red, blue, green, orange, and for the items that really prodded at her, a bright fuchsia she didn't care for but that stood out the most. Where colors intersected, meaning two seemingly independent items connected, she marked the squares with a black *X*.

She plowed her way through all of the data, going on pure gut instinct now, until she had a two-page table that looked like a child's coloring book. Now that she had all her data in one place, she pored over it, looking for any kind of pattern, anything that triggered a revelation, however small.

When she at last looked up and glanced at the clock, it was after 11:00 p.m. And she still hadn't come up with a new idea, or a new way of putting the old ideas together to make sense of them.

As an experiment, she copied her grid to another page and rearranged it all so that the colors were all lumped together. Sometimes a new way of looking at things sparked ideas. She settled in for another session. It seemed as if she'd only begun when a knock on the door startled her out of her concentration.

A quick glance at the clock told her it was just after midnight. Wariness jolted through her as she wondered who'd be at her hotel room door at this hour. Grabbing up the holster she'd removed for comfort and slipping the Glock out, she padded in sock feet over to the door to peer through the security peephole.

An unexpected heat replaced the wariness in a rolling sweep.

Justin.

She flipped off the dead bolt, undid the chain and yanked the door open.

For a moment she forgot to breathe. She simply stood there, staring. Sometimes, she thought, *I forget how incredibly gorgeous he is. I keep thinking those eyes can't really be that color, that the air can't really crackle around him because he's so damned alive. And every time I'm wrong.*

Maybe you're wrong about a lot of things when it comes to this man.

That was the loudest that little gut-level voice had ever been, and she knew she wouldn't be able to ignore it much longer.

"Hi," he said.

She would have hugged him, but his hands were full. She settled for a quick kiss of what cheek was available behind the unexpected spray of beautiful pale orange and white lilies he was holding. The spicy scent tickled her nose, and almost involuntarily she drew in a deep breath.

"What are you doing here?" she asked as she stepped back and held the door for him.

"Did I forget to mention we deliver?" he asked as he came in and nudged the door shut behind him with one heel. Alex redid the latch and then watched with no little bemusement as Justin unloaded his cargo onto the only clear surface in the room, the king-size bed.

"I'm glad you're still up," he added as he set his briefcase down on the floor beside the bed.

"I've been working."

"I see that," he said, looking at the table covered with papers and her laptop. "Too hard, no doubt."

She found herself smiling at his solicitous tone. Then she gestured at the bed. "What's all this?"

"First, flowers that reminded me of you," he said as he filled the ice bucket with water and plopped the richly scented flowers into it. That the colors were reminiscent of her hair and skin was a fact not lost on her, and it warmed her in a way she'd not felt before.

"Then," he said, picking up a box that was exuding a marvelous aroma and nudging aside a stack of papers on the dresser to make room for it, "there are some very evil cinnamon rolls, suitable for midnight snacking, that I was unable to fight off in the airport."

Her stomach reminded her suddenly and sharply that she'd missed dinner. "Bless you," she said, meaning it.

"And then we have a special delivery," he said, drawing an envelope out of a side pocket of his brief-case. He handed it to her and, curiously, she took it. She recognized the handwriting on the front immediately. G.C. Her gaze flicked immediately to Justin's face.

"He's not angry, is he?"

"With you? Of course not. I'd say he understands his granddaughter better than anyone."

She relaxed slightly. "I was only trying to protect him."

"He knows that. He just doesn't need it."

She gave him a sideways look. "You sound pretty certain of that."

"I told you, we had a nice, long talk."

"Do I want to know what about?"

"Probably not," he said blithely.

Deciding that was best left right there, she tore open the envelope to read the enclosed note. G.C. did understand her, that much was clear, but he also told her if she ever tried to protect him like that again he'd throttle her. She grinned. She could just hear him saying it, trying to convince her he meant it. He closed with his love, and a PS that read, "You've got it right this time."

There was no further clarification, and she felt a bit puzzled. If he was chastising her for trying to protect him, what had she gotten right?

But then she noticed Justin bending to dig into his briefcase on the floor. She'd put that tautly muscled backside up against any in the world, Alex thought as she looked at him. He moved so beautifully. With all the grace and leashed power of blooded horse.

Her own analogy to the animals she so loved to ride, silent though it was, made her blush. And the heat that had been building in her ever since he'd knocked on the door began to pool somewhere low and deep, making her ache softly.

"Here's what you really want," he said, his tone clearly teasing as he straightened again with a lengthy computer printout in his hands.

If I told you what *I* really wanted right now, we wouldn't get to that until morning, she thought.

He went very still. As if she'd spoken out loud. As, judging by the warmth in her cheeks and what she guessed must be showing in her face, she might as well have.

"Alex," he said, his voice suddenly low and harsh.

And then she was in his arms, kissing him with all the hunger that had built since she'd realized she was being a fool to resist something so strong, so right.

Pressed against his chest, she felt his heart begin to race, felt as much as heard the sudden hammering. That his pulse leaped as hers had both thrilled and reassured her. No matter what happened from here on, she was not in this alone, this was not one-sided, this was a man of heart and soul and passion, unlike Emerson—

She shoved the last crumbling memories of her ex-fiancé out of her mind, realizing even as she did that they were likely going to be burned to ashes in the next few minutes. He had never, ever made her feel the way Justin made her feel.

"I hope you brought something else in that magic bag of tricks," she whispered against his lips. "Something from a drugstore?"

"From the airport gift shop," he confessed, sounding more than a little breathless.

"That'll do."

"You're sure? Once we start, it's going to be a runaway train, and I can't promise I can stop it."

"I won't ask you to. This has been a long time coming."

He groaned in assent, muttered "Damn long," under his breath, but took her mouth voraciously with his before she could react. He kissed her again and again, long and probing, tasting, until she couldn't help but push closer and closer, moving, rubbing herself against him. And then he was pulling at her clothes, and she at his.

When they were naked, he looked at her with a flattering expression of awe on his face. An expression, she guessed, that was echoed on her own face. He was even more beautiful than she'd imagined, truly the Dark Angel of her youth come to maturity: strong, muscular, perfectly put together. And incredibly aroused.

He made a quick move to grab a small box from a pocket of his discarded jeans, took out a foil envelope and dropped the box on the bed.

"Wait," she whispered when he moved to open it.

She reached for him, wanting to touch him before he was sheathed, wanting to trace the length and breadth of him with hands too long denied.

He shifted slightly, making it easier for her. And the low, husky groan he let out at the first touch of her fingers only fired her higher, hotter, quicker. He grabbed her shoulders, his fingers tightening as she stroked him. When she reached farther below and cupped him, he gasped and let his head loll back as if his muscles were suddenly too weak to hold it up.

And then, as if he'd borne as much as he could, he pulled her to him, his head lifting and then coming down on her like some fierce raptor on his prey. His lips touched her and never lifted as he tasted her, her lips, her cheek, her ear, down her throat, over her collarbone.

She was panting by the time he reached her breast, arching her back, begging him to find that taut, begging peak that was tightening in anticipation of the hot wetness of his mouth.

He reached it, drew her nipple in and flicked it with his tongue. She cried out at the sweet shock of sensation, and then again when his lips tightened and he sucked, first gently, and then, as she trembled, harder.

She'd expected it to be good. Better than good, she'd expected fantastic. She'd known it would be, simply by the effect he had on her every time she'd ever even thought about sex with him.

She'd never expected it to be shattering. And so early, before they'd done much more than kiss and touch. She wondered if she would be able to stand going further, if her body wouldn't simply fly apart long before they came together completely.

She'd also never expected to completely lose herself. She'd always thought she never would, that she would always maintain some modicum of control. An Athena would, wouldn't she?

That theory went out the window as he moved to her other breast. And then nothing else mattered. There was no nervousness, no wariness, no fear, there was only Justin and his mouth and his hands and his body against hers.

For one brief moment he broke contact, drew back enough to look at her face. He didn't speak, and after a moment she did.

"Let's take the brakes off this train."

His mouth curved into that crooked grin she loved. "Spoken like a true Athena," he said.

And that simply, she had the answer. In the same

way as they threw themselves into life, searching out and following their passion, Athenas would settle for nothing else—nothing less—in their personal lives.

It was why she hadn't married Emerson.

It was why she was here now with Justin.

The last of her reservations were seared to ash as they tumbled down to the bed. He sheathed himself hastily, and Alex felt herself quiver in anticipation and undiluted eagerness. For the first time in her life she was not only ready but wild for it, for him, for this man, at this time. Now. Right now.

She didn't realize she'd said those last words aloud until he went still for a moment.

"No brakes?"

"No brakes," she agreed fervently, arching herself up to him.

He swore, low and soft and nearly hoarse. He moved quickly then, almost quickly enough to satisfy her need. He was over her, probing, searching, and before he could she reached to guide him. And then he was in her, driving hard and deep, and Alex cried out at the perfection of it, the joy of being at last united, utterly filled with the man she'd half feared didn't exist in this world.

The rhythm he set was both too slow and too fast, and she clawed at him in near desperation. She heard him say her name, once, twice and then a third time in a guttural exclamation that was the last bit of impetus she needed. Her body clenched violently, releasing all the need she'd stored up for so long in one fierce contraction, wrenching another exclamation from him. It blended with her own cry of his name as everything became clear to her in one blinding flash of power and sensation.

Alex had heard the phone ring, but then it had gone away, so she'd drifted back off. Or started to. After a moment the sound of a voice speaking softly made it through the sweet haze she was in. But listening was beyond her after a long, passionate night in the arms of the Dark Angel that had involved exploring, touching, savoring, tenderness alternating with hot, driving, pure sex.

And the occasional cinnamon roll.

She turned over, eyes still closed, her body feeling wonderfully, pleasantly used, as if she'd only now discovered its true purpose.

Or at least its capacity for tremendous sex, she thought wryly as she grew more awake.

Then the male voice stopped, and when she heard the sound of the phone receiver being replaced, she finally opened her eyes.

Justin, just as gorgeous, and still as naked as he'd been in her arms all night, was propped against a pillow, looking at...nothing, apparently.

He did not look happy.

She pulled herself up on one elbow. "Justin?"

His gaze shifted, and she realized with unpleasant certainty it was her he wasn't happy with.

"That was Kayla. What an…illuminating phone call."

She sat up then, knowing from his tone she wasn't going to like this.

"So," he said, an unmistakable edge in his voice, "you trust me enough to sleep with me, but not enough to tell me somebody tried to kill you?"

Uh-oh, she thought.

It was going to be one of *those* morning afters.

Chapter 11

"Was that what changed your mind?" Justin's voice was edgy, tight. "You had a narrow escape, so you decided it was time for us to have sex, in case next time you didn't make it?"

Alex sighed. "I hope you know me better than that."

After he'd first spoken, she'd needed the armor of clothes. She rolled out of bed, pulled her pants and T-shirt back on, jammed her fingers through her hair and then sat cross-legged on the bed, facing him.

Now she considered her words carefully, not used to discussions like this that were about so much more than they appeared to be on the surface. She dis-

The Silhouette Reader Service™ — Here's how it works:

Accepting your 2 free books and mystery gift places you under no obligation to buy anything. You may keep the books and gift and return the shipping statement marked "cancel." If you do not cancel, about a month later we'll send you 4 additional books and bill you just $3.99 each in the U.S., or $4.47 each in Canada, plus 25¢ shipping & handling per book and applicable taxes if any.* That's the complete price and — compared to cover prices of $4.99 each in the U.S., and $5.99 each in Canada — it's quite a bargain! You may cancel at any time, but if you choose to continue, every month we'll send you 4 more books which you may either purchase at the discount price or return to us and cancel your subscription.

*Terms and prices subject to change without notice. Sales tax applicable in N.Y. Canadian residents will be charged applicable provincial taxes and GST. Credit or debit balances in a customer's account(s) may be offset by any other outstanding balance owed by or to the customer.

If offer card is missing write to: The Silhouette Reader Service, 3010 Walden Ave., P.O. Box 1867, Buffalo, NY 14240-1867

NO POSTAGE
NECESSARY
IF MAILED
IN THE
UNITED STATES

BUSINESS REPLY MAIL
FIRST-CLASS MAIL   PERMIT NO. 717-003   BUFFALO, NY

POSTAGE WILL BE PAID BY ADDRESSEE

SILHOUETTE READER SERVICE
3010 WALDEN AVE
PO BOX 1867
BUFFALO NY 14240-9952

Play the

Lucky Hearts Game

and get...

2 FREE BOOKS
and a **FREE MYSTERY GIFT...**

Yes!

YOURS to KEEP!

I have scratched off the silver card. Please send me my *2 FREE BOOKS* and *FREE mystery GIFT*. I understand that I am under no obligation to purchase any books as explained on the back of this card.

Scratch Here!

then look below to see what your cards get you...
2 Free Books & a Free Mystery Gift!

▲ DETACH AND MAIL CARD TODAY! ▲

300 SDL EFX9

FIRST NAME

200 SDL EFWX

LAST NAME

ADDRESS

APT.#

CITY

STATE/PROV.

ZIP/POSTAL CODE

(SL-B-04/06)

Twenty-one gets you
2 FREE BOOKS
and a *FREE MYSTERY GIFT!*

Twenty gets you
2 FREE BOOKS!

Nineteen gets you
1 FREE BOOK!

TRY AGAIN!

Offer limited to one per household and not valid to current Silhouette Bombshell® subscribers. All orders subject to approval. Please allow 4-6 weeks for delivery.

carded one approach after another, until finally she simply told him the whole story.

He listened impassively, arms crossed, and she wasn't sure if her explanation was going to change a thing about his reaction. Of course, sitting there talking to a man who was still gorgeously naked beneath the covers wasn't the most calming experience of her life. Especially when she'd just had outrageously hot, killer sex for the first time in her life, with that man.

She managed to get it all out, finally. She wasn't sure how clear she'd been, but it was the best she could do under the circumstances. When she was done filling him in on what had happened out in the desert, she took a breath, hesitated, then plunged ahead to try and explain why she hadn't contacted him.

"I could say there wasn't time to call you after what happened. I could say there was no point in calling you since there was nothing you could do from D.C. I could say I had it under control. I could say that when you got here there were…other things on my mind. And all of it would be true."

Leaning against the hotel headboard, arms crossed over his bare chest, looking more like some warrior caught midbattle than the legendary Dark Angel of Athena, Justin just looked at her, waiting. He wasn't, it was clear, going to make this easy on her.

"If I didn't know that what you're suggesting does happen, and often," she said, "I'd be insulted. But I do know, so I'll just say I had chosen long before I went out for a ride. It came too quickly for it not to have been in the back of my mind the whole time. I just didn't realize it until I was face-to-face with the possibility of the choice being taken away from me."

He appeared to ponder this, his expression shifting from edgy to thoughtful. But when he still didn't say anything, Alex sighed again and rubbed at the back of her neck.

"You know, some men wouldn't look a gift horse in the mouth."

"Some men aren't thinking forever," Justin retorted.

Alex blinked. "And you are?"

"You're not?"

She simply stared at him. She couldn't think of a single thing to say. She hadn't dared think of forever with him. She'd been so wrong about Emerson, letting herself be swept along on the considerable tide of her mother's approval, something she'd never had in her life before. It had been unlike her, completely, and she knew she'd be eternally grateful that she'd awakened in time. And always amazed that she had let it go so far.

But it had also shaken her faith in her judgment. She no longer trusted—

"…we had a nice, long talk," Justin had said.

"You've got it right this time," her grandfather had written.

And suddenly she understood what G.C. had been talking about. He hadn't been talking about her protectiveness of him, but about Justin. Giving him his seal of approval, something Emerson, for all his medical genius, had never earned.

Justin wasn't Emerson, she thought.

And she wasn't her mother.

"I've been afraid to think of forever," she said quietly.

Justin drew back slightly. "Afraid? You?"

The astonishment in his voice was somehow flattering. "I've been wrong before."

"Haven't we all? Or are Athena women not allowed that human failing?"

"I just haven't been wrong very often." She grimaced. "That sounds awful. I don't mean it that way."

"It sounds true. You are who you are," he said, his voice sounding wry and admiring at the same time. The tone enabled her to go on.

"And when I have been wrong, it's almost always in my personal life."

"Unlike me, who tends to screw up across the board," he said with a grin, that killer, heart-levitating grin that told her she was forgiven.

"That's one of the things I...love about you. You live with such...gusto."

His amusement faded as he looked at her. "Alex," he said softly. "You—"

The ringing of the room phone made her inevitably think of the phrase "saved by the bell." Except she didn't feel saved, she felt interrupted at a crucial moment. So she was a bit sharp when she answered.

"Bad time?"

"Allison? No, no, I'm sorry. It's fine. You got my message?"

She had called Allison during one of her short breaks during her marathon yesterday. As always when she called Marion's daughter, she got only a cryptic voice mail menu. Allison had so many irons in the fire it was hard to keep track, but Alex had always suspected her sister Athenian—who had also been Rainy's best friend—was up to far bigger things than any of them realized.

"Yes. I'm sorry it took me a while to get back to you. I've still been tied up on something critical. But you said you found something new about my mother?"

Quickly Alex explained the relevant details.

"Blackmailed? My mother?" Allison sounded doubtful, but went on. "I don't remember anything that might fit that scenario, but I've seen and heard too much by now to totally discount the possibility that anybody could be a target."

Alex knew she was referring to the mess last year that had threatened to embroil Athena in chaos.

"I'd rather not ask my father, talking about Mom still upsets him so. But I'll talk to my brother, see if it fits with anything he knew."

"And the spider drawing?"

"Now there you've got me stumped. My mother never doodled, that I remember. If she drew it, and repeatedly, it means something."

"That's what I thought."

"Have you talked to anyone else?"

"Justin's helping. And I asked Tory if the spider meant anything to her, told her why I was asking. She was on another line with Sam, so she may have told her. That's it."

"No one outside Athena, then."

"No." She liked the way Allison included Justin in that group. She thought he would, too.

"That's good. Let's keep it among us for now."

Alex agreed.

"Is there anything I can do to help from my end?" Allison asked.

"I was wondering if you had any of your mother's papers? I know the official ones are in the Athena Library, but…"

"I think I might," Allison said. "Some notes, letters, that kind of thing?"

"Yes. I know what you have would likely be more…personal, but if you wouldn't mind?"

"You're trying to find out the truth about what happened to her, why would I mind? I'll find what I have and call you to find out where to ship them when I do."

"Thank you for trusting me with them," Alex said.

"You're an Athenian," was all Allison said.

And it was, Alex knew, all that needed to be said.

As they hung up, she heard the rustling behind her,

and turned in time to see Justin finish zipping his jeans and reach for his shirt.

Too bad, she thought. The view was spectacular.

"I'd much prefer we resume our previous activities," he said, "but I suspect your mind is already up and running elsewhere."

"Justin—"

He stopped her with a shake of his head. "Later. Right now I need to get home, unpack, check in. Then we'll talk about what we're going to do about this little situation you've stirred up."

She opened her mouth to question the "we" part, then closed it again. She wasn't going to commit the insult of halfheartedness, not now. Not after last night.

"All right," she said, as meekly as she could manage.

Justin laughed. "And that's what I love about you," he said. "Once you make up your mind, it's damn the torpedoes."

He said it so easily, that word love, as if he'd been saying it in his mind for a very long time. And that he knew her that well made it all the sweeter to hear.

He pulled her to him and kissed her, long and thoroughly. And then, while she was still a bit wobbly from that, he pulled open the door and looked back at her. "Think about moving out of here," he said. "Two of us can guard better than one."

And then he was gone, leaving her to realize a few seconds later that he'd meant for her to move to his place. She'd only been there once, but the apartment had left an impression. Less than three miles from the FBI Phoenix headquarters, it was convenient, spacious and, perhaps not accidentally, reminded her of a reinforced bunker with concrete walls and landscaping that consisted mostly of small stones and cactus.

For eyes more used to rolling green hills it was quite a contrast, just as Athena had been. Although she'd grown rather fond of cactus of late.

She also remembered the second bedroom was in use as a home office, full of books and computer gear. Which left his bed.

Or the leather couch, she thought. Which seemed rather ridiculous in light of last night. And the thought of night after night like that took her breath away.

And at that moment the rest of the quote Justin had used came to her. Admiral Farragut had indeed said "Damn the torpedoes." But he'd followed it with "Full speed ahead!"

"All right, then," she said aloud. "Full speed ahead it is."

And she began to plan her packing.

"Right there," Alex said.

They were seated at Justin's now-cluttered dining table in the alcove that looked out at the gravel and cactus garden. He reached for the pad she'd pointed at, that held her notes from the original file on Marion's murder.

"It's only my notes from reading the original," she told him. "Eric couldn't let the original file out of his custody, and I didn't want to get him into trouble."

"Eric?"

"Eric Hunt. He's the detective who handled the case originally."

Justin leaned back in his chair. He'd been clearly startled when she'd so easily agreed to staying with him here. Startled but pleased. So was she, actually. If nothing else, she'd learned that while he wasn't a slob, he wasn't a neat freak either—nothing was out of control, but the place looked comfortably lived in.

So far it had gone well. Of course, so far all it had been was more of what she'd been doing for what seemed like days, going over the same data over and over, twisting, turning, squeezing, always hoping something new would fall out.

Tonight might be a different story. The hotel had been neutral territory of a sort; his bed was something else. But she'd worry about that when the time came.

"Good luck reading them," she added, gesturing at the notes. "I was kind of in a hurry."

"I'll manage," he said, and picked up the yellow legal pad.

She watched him for a moment, watched those amazing-colored eyes dart so quickly she wondered how he could be taking anything in. But she was under no delusion that his mind wasn't just as quick, and she turned back to her sorting.

He finished her notes, then started on the list of names from Marion's prosecutorial days, and then her county attorney cases. Alex stayed silent, hoping he would come up with some brilliant answer to it all.

A couple hours later Justin stood up and stretched. Alex looked up at him.

"One of the few things I remember about my dad," he said unexpectedly, "is a story he told me when I was little, about an old hunting dog his father used to have. Dumb as a post, he said, and always barking up the wrong tree. By the time he figured out he was wrong, the quarry had long ago moved on."

Alex leaned back in her chair. "I'm sure this seeming non sequitur isn't one. You think we're looking in the wrong place."

He nodded. "Seems too…obvious. And while that's often the right place to look, it doesn't feel like it in this case."

"Because?"

He shrugged. "Marion Gracelyn was too complicated a woman to die for a reason as simple as payback."

Alex let out a compressed breath. "I've been feeling the same way."

Justin leaned over and picked up the computer printout he'd brought with him from D.C., which had been forgotten in the passion of last night.

"I think we should start looking here."

He dropped the stack of pages in front of her. She knew what it was. It was exactly what he'd promised, the senatorial records of—judging by the size of the stack—just about everything Senator Marion Gracelyn had been involved with.

"I started going through it at the airport and on the plane," he said. "I red-marked anything that seemed unimportant, like votes in which she was just one of the majority, no reason for her to be singled out. Or part of a committee that sent things along, one vote on a panel. I highlighted anything she was the front person for. And circled which ones of those caused any…unrest."

"You *started* going through it?" Alex said, amazed.

"It's a long wait and a long flight."

This reminded her of something she'd been meaning to ask. "Wasn't your training seminar supposed to go through today?"

He lifted one shoulder negligently. "Today was just the handing out of certificates, patting each other on the back and some drinking. I decided to pass." His lips twitched. "I ended up having a lot more fun."

She lowered her gaze, hoping to avoid the blush she felt rising in her cheeks.

"And I'm sure you have an explanation for your boss in the morning."

"Don't need one. I'm taking time off."

She looked up quickly. "What?"

"You heard me."

"Justin, if this is because of me—"

"You'll live with it. Or take it up with your grandfather."

"G.C.? What's he got to do with—" She stopped short as realization struck. "Is *that* what you two were talking about?"

"Some of the time. But get used to it. I promised him I'd be on you like skin."

That was a simile she could have done without at the moment. It brought to mind too many hot, vivid memories from last night.

"I didn't tell him exactly how I hoped that would work out, though," he said, as if he'd read her mind.

And if he *had* read your mind, she thought, would it surprise you?

Not at this point, she decided. Nothing Justin Cohen said or did in the way of perception would surprise her anymore.

"I don't need a bodyguard," she said.

"No one said you did. But two trained observers are better than one, right?"

She couldn't argue with that.

"Besides, it got you here, didn't it? How do you know that wasn't the whole idea? That I didn't just manipulate the situation to get you here, and into my bed?"

"Because you don't work that way." She dismissed the idea instantly.

A look crossed his face that she couldn't begin to describe. "I don't?"

"Of course not. You wouldn't want a woman you

had to manipulate. Or, for that matter, one who would let herself be manipulated like that."

That odd look was followed by a long, slow smile that did ridiculous things to her stomach.

"Thanks," he said softly.

"For what?" she said, embarrassed by her own reactions.

"For knowing that. And for knowing it without even having to think about it."

He kissed her then, and it was a while before she got back to work, while Justin ordered Chinese takeout. After it arrived, she took her first real look at the printout he'd brought.

"I know that's just the highlights," Justin said, gesturing with his chopsticks at the papers spread out on his table. "If you want more details, it'll take more digging."

Alex nodded as she plucked a shrimp out of her rice lunch combo. "Marion left her official senatorial papers to the Athena Library. I'll call Christine to set up access."

Justin gave her a sideways look over his carton of sweet-and-sour pork. "Can I come?"

She blinked. "To Athena?"

He nodded, a grin curving his mouth. "I think I'd like to see it without having to sneak around."

She couldn't help laughing. "You've done your share of that, all right. Okay, I'll take you along. The return of the Dark Angel and all that."

He rolled his eyes. "Oh, please."

"Hey, don't mess with the fantasy."

He set down his chopsticks. "Is that what I am? A fantasy?"

Alex snorted, rather inelegantly. Her mother would be appalled. "You can ask this of the woman you've worn out in the past twelve hours? Fantastic, yes, but fantasy? Hardly. You're real, Agent Cohen. One hundred percent. Lucky for me."

He stared at her for a long, silent moment. And the expression that crept over his face made her smile.

"You do have a way with words," he said. "I've never wanted to have raging sex on my kitchen table before."

Images slammed through her mind, vivid, erotic memories of last night, leading to equally vivid imaginings about what he'd just said. Herself, sprawled naked on the glass table, like some banquet laid out for him to take.

And him taking her.

Hot and fierce, with that driving, hard body that filled her beyond measure, beyond pleasure, beyond joy.

Justin took one look at her face and sucked in a harsh breath. "Alex," he whispered, in that same gravelly voice she'd heard so often during the night, when he kissed her, when he stroked her, when he shivered beneath her hands on him, when he sank into her. That gravelly voice that sent sensations she'd never felt before, sensations she never guessed she could feel, rippling through her.

Blood surged through her in hot, heavy beats, and in a matter of seconds she thought she might die if they didn't do exactly what he'd suggested.

So they did.

Chapter 12

"Ah, the Dark Angel returns to Athena."

To his credit, Justin didn't groan when Christine greeted them with the teasing comment.

"Through the front door in the daylight this time," he said. "At least you didn't say 'to the scene of the crime,'" he added.

"I thought about it," the older woman said with a laugh.

"Thank you for holding back, then," Justin said, grinning at her. Alex smiled to herself; she liked that he was so at ease with the entire concept and with the reality of Athena. Anything less would be a stumbling block she wasn't sure they could get past.

"I didn't say it because I don't really think of it as a crime," Christine said. "You were just trying to do what had to be done."

Alex watched his face change, and smiled inwardly at the surprise in his expression.

"Thank you," he said.

Christine shook her head. "You were part of unraveling a mystery that could have threatened Athena's very existence. We owe you thanks."

"And now," Alex put in when she saw Justin struggling with what to say to that, "we're trying to solve another Athena mystery."

"Of course. Marion's papers." She got to her feet. "Come along, I've brought them into my den. The girls need access to the library, and I was afraid you'd be too much of a distraction."

"You mean the Dark Angel would be," Alex teased.

Christine looked back at them. "You both would. And together you make quite a couple. The colors alone are striking."

She supposed the Athena principal was right. Justin's dark hair next to her own red-gold locks made an attention-getting combination just because of the contrast. But she still harbored the suspicion that among the female students here, it would be Justin who drew the most interest. And she certainly couldn't blame them for that.

"Besides," Christine added to Alex, a wickedly impish expression on her face, "don't think the Dark

Angel legend hasn't grown. You're part of it now, too. It's unbearably romantic, how the girl who saw him all those years ago is now—"

"Oh, Lord," Alex muttered, waving her to silence with a protesting hand.

Christine laughed, and Alex thought how much happier she sounded now than she had during the chaos last year. Another side benefit of solving that far-reaching conspiracy: Christine had finally been able to put her own small, unwitting part in it behind her.

"I had another thought, as well," Christine said as they went into the cozy den of her campus bungalow.

The room was lined with bookcases except for one corner that held a roomy computer desk. Centered there was a large flat-screen monitor that seemed oddly angled to Alex until she remembered it was probably adjusted that way for Christine's lack of vision in her left eye because of a training accident years ago that had ended the former Army captain's military career.

"What was that?" Alex asked in response to Christine's comment.

"Marion often accessed her e-mail from here, when she would visit. Because my machine is regularly checked and secure, I don't think she worried much about confidentiality. You might be able to access those files." She shrugged. "I could never bring myself to delete them."

Alex thought of her sister Cassandra Samantha St. John, who so often had said, "Nothing's ever truly deleted from a computer hard drive." Sam was a computer whiz who could find things underneath things underneath things on any computer, anywhere.

Hopefully this wouldn't require that kind of skill, because, although she was fairly good, Alex knew she didn't have that kind of knack or knowledge. But if they needed it, she knew Sam would come running in a heartbeat.

"Do you remember anything unusual about the time she was killed?" Alex asked.

"It's all a little foggy, I'm afraid," Christine admitted. "I was so shocked. They asked me if she'd done anything out of the ordinary recently, or said anything. Other than being here a bit more than usual, she hadn't—not that I'd noticed, anyway."

"How did she seem to you, in those last days?"

"Wired," Christine said frankly. "Wound up. But then, that was Marion. She was never a serene person to be around in any case."

"Any more so than usual, then? Like maybe there was something more specific she was focused on?"

Christine looked thoughtful. "Perhaps. She did seem a little more…intense, maybe. But she always was, so if there was something really wrong, I'm not sure I would have noticed a difference."

Christine left them alone to work, and she and Justin quickly divided up the items to slog through with an ease that pleased Alex. It *was* good to have help on this, she thought.

Even if it is a test of my self-discipline to keep my mind on the task at hand, she added to herself, keeping her eyes on the stack of letters she had before her.

The work of being a senator, Alex soon realized, was vast, varied, and complex. She was amazed at the things people wrote to complain about, and expected someone on the level of a U.S. senator to handle.

She was even more amazed at the number of those petty things Marion Gracelyn had actually handled.

It didn't take long for them to figure out the method Marion had used to organize things. Topics, issues and legislation were grouped individually and then chronologically within those separate files. It was supremely easy to follow any one issue or problem from beginning to end, perfect for their purposes and much easier than if they'd been filed in chronological order only.

Alex read as quickly as she could while still being thorough, making notes of anything that seemed to have left anyone unhappy. However positive or constructive something was, it seemed like there was always somebody who didn't like it. And there were a few somebodys who seemed to have made a hobby out of not liking it, no matter what the "it" was.

"Some people just say no to everything," she muttered, making notes of the names that kept popping up.

"I've never been able to figure out if those types think they know better than the rest of us or just don't like *any* idea, no matter how good, if it's not their own," Justin said, clearly finding more of the same in the stack of stuff he was going through.

"Problem is they don't have any good ideas of their own," Alex said, then laughed. "Gads, I sound like G.C. watching the evening news."

"Good for you," Justin said. "He's a wise man."

She glanced up, then. He wasn't looking at her but at the papers in front of him, so she had a chance to watch him unobserved for a moment. And as she did, the wonder of what had happened between them struck her anew.

She may have been a fool for a long time, dragging her feet with him, she thought, but she was certainly over it now.

I am *so* over it, she thought, and lowered her head again to mask her grin in case he looked up.

"So," Alex said as they drove back toward downtown Phoenix, "we have a longer list of names."

"Including every obstructionist in the state of Arizona, I'd bet."

Alex laughed. "Scary part is some of them are in office now. G.C. would be gagging."

"At a guess I'd say most of them are harmless," Justin said. "At least, when it comes to something like murder. They seem more the letter-writing, demonstrating, get-my-name/cause/photo-in-the-paper types."

"I tend to agree." She sighed. "Too bad guess-work doesn't hold up in court."

Justin laughed. "Wouldn't our lives be so much easier if it did?"

"I think those three we found in the e-mail records might lead somewhere, though."

"The save-the-Gila-monster guy caught my eye," Justin said.

"Me, too. Especially since they're hardly endangered. Made me wonder if he was talking about poison in a broader sense."

The exchange of e-mails had been entertaining at first, but toward the end, it had taken on a faintly threatening tone.

"Anybody who'd keep them as pets isn't wrapped real tight anyway," Justin said. "Look, let's give it a rest for a bit, okay? We've done nothing but dig through this stuff all day. We need to let it perk for a while."

She was more than happy to agree. When he proposed a nice steak dinner after the day of poring over the papers that were supposed to have been made obsolete with the coming of the computer, she said yes immediately.

They stopped by his place to change clothes when he told her the place he had in mind frowned on jeans for dinner. She was ready quickly, since she had a very limited choice of wardrobe. She'd only brought one dress. It was a basic black sleeveless that she could accessorize like mad, to make it look different each time she wore it. This time she added only a colorful scarf, dangling earrings and a gold-and-diamond pendent G.C. had given her upon her graduation from the FBI Academy.

"You're an agent now, and I'm immensely proud of you," he'd said, "but I don't want you to ever forget you're also a beautiful woman."

She caught her hair up in a knot in the back, leaving a few tendrils down to frame her face, and did a touch-up on her makeup. When she came out of the bathroom, Justin looked up from the piece of newspaper he was reading. He went very still.

"Wow," he said, sounding a bit wobbly.

Apparently, he agreed with G.C., Alex thougnt, with a spurt of purely feminine pleasure she hadn't felt in a long time.

"You're going to ruin the scientist stereotype," he added, beginning to smile.

"You clean up nice, too," she said with a grin.

He laughed, and offered her his arm in a rather grandiose manner.

The restaurant was elegant, the wine smooth and heady, the steak done to absolute perfection. Yet it all paled beside Alex's sudden anticipation of the night to come. She'd never been like this, never felt like this with a man. She didn't know if that was good or bad, only that as strongly as her gut had warned her to go cautiously before, it was now screaming this was right.

Very right.

She tried to make herself concentrate on the incredible amount of data they'd accumulated, hoping that somehow the solution would suddenly pop up and become obvious.

"I hereby declare a moratorium on work talk," Justin declared, as if he'd again read her mind.

"It's not work," she reminded him. "At least, not official work."

"Splitting hairs that are already split, Agent Forsythe," he said with mock sternness, gesturing at her with his wineglass.

She couldn't help but chuckle at him. "So what shall we talk about? The weather? Politics? Religion?"

"Going to get hotter…dirty…and lapsed. You?"

The chuckle became a laugh. "At least it's not humid…*dirty*'s too nice a word…and intermittent," she said, and got a laugh in return.

He looked at her for a moment then, a long silent moment that made her blood start to heat.

"It's about that pink elephant," he said softly, a wry smile curving his lips.

She didn't pretend to misunderstand. "The one we're not supposed to notice or think about? Yeah. Takes up a lot of room, doesn't it?"

"Heart and mind," he said. "But let's drop it there, or I'm going to insult the chef by dragging you out of here in the middle of your dinner."

There was little conversation after that, and Alex wryly noted they were both eating rather quickly.

When they were finished, Justin paid quickly—and tipped generously, she noticed—and they walked out into the balmy evening air.

When they reached his bureau car, the stereotypical black four-door sedan, he walked her to the passenger door, opened it and turned to her. He gripped her shoulders. Started to pull her to him. She read his intent in his eyes, and her lips parted in anticipation.

"No," he said suddenly.

She blinked.

"If I start now, I'll be in agony all the way home. Let's go."

"Fast," she said, feeling breathless.

"You can bet on it," he muttered, as he walked around to the driver's side.

Alex was trying not to think, but her body seemed to have taken charge in that department. She managed not to look at her watch every block, but barely. She rolled down her window, thinking the air in her face might help. That wouldn't be possible in another couple months, it would be far too warm not to have the air-conditioning on.

The fresh air helped. But after a few moments she began to realize that she was hearing something odd. A very light, irregular tapping sound that seemed tied to the roughness of the road.

She glanced at Justin. He was sitting behind the wheel with his head cocked slightly, as if listening.

"You hear it, too?"

"I'm hearing something," he said. "Very faint, but it's there. Like a wire's loose or something."

He pulled off the street at the next opportunity, which happened to be the driveway of a large office complex. He left the car running but set the brake. Her instincts were yelling, and she suspected his were, too. She slung her purse over her shoulder and got out at the same time he did.

She looked over her side of the car. Saw nothing unusual. Bent to peer underneath. Saw something white dangling from the undercarriage. Plastic. Wide. Familiar.

A zip tie. Holding something—

She jerked upright.

"Bomb!"

Chapter 13

Alex whirled, dived at Justin. He didn't question, he just reacted. He caught her around the waist and they swung backward together. The impetus drove them toward, and then behind the large Dumpster that appeared to be awaiting emptying.

She barely had time to catch her breath before the world tilted. An explosion of sound and light and concussion hammered at her eyes and ears. And moments later the awful smell of an evil kind of smoke scoured at her nose.

She didn't have to look around the corner of their improvised metal barricade to know that but for their highly trained instincts and quick reactions they would both be dead.

"Are you all right?"

Justin's voice was brusque, controlled, but she heard the undertone of worry and liked it.

"I'm fine. You?"

"Intact," he said as he got to his feet and held down a hand to help her up.

They stepped out from behind the shelter of the Dumpster. The car was engulfed in flames shooting fifteen feet in the air, and the smell of burning vinyl and carpet thick and choking.

And probably toxic, Alex thought as she coughed.

"What did you see?"

Alex turned to look at him. In the staccato, rapid-fire manner of an official report, she told him.

"White, heavy-duty zip-tie—the end of it was what was tapping against the undercarriage—holding a wrapped package to the frame. Digital timer on the outside, three wires going into the package."

He sucked in a breath and his lips tightened.

"If he'd used a lighter weight tie that I wouldn't have heard, if he hadn't been just that little bit sloppy and had trimmed the loose end…" she began, emotion creeping into her voice now.

"And if you hadn't rolled down your window in the first place," he said, his expression grim as he put into words what they both knew; they'd been damned lucky.

Sirens sounded in the distance, and they both knew they were in for some explaining.

Alex's gaze locked with his, saw that he was thinking, as was she, of what would not be happening in the next few hours.

It was going to be a very long night.

"Do you have any idea how much paperwork having a bureau car blow up on you causes?"

To get home they'd borrowed another vehicle from the small pool available. It was an older one, scheduled for retirement soon, and it showed. At the slightest bump, something seemed to rattle, each time from a different quarter.

But at this predawn hour, traffic was very light, and it wouldn't be a lengthy drive back to his apartment. And there they had her rental if they needed something more reliable.

Assuming nobody'd gotten to it, too.

"No," Alex said in answer to his half-rhetorical question. "But I know how much paperwork breaking a brand-new electron microscope causes, which is probably something similar."

"Probably."

He sounded beyond glum. Justin, she realized with an inward grin, was capable of near whining. For some reason, she wasn't sure why, that pleased her. She'd have to figure that out someday.

But not now.

"It's not like you parked the car next to a burning

fireworks plant or something," she teased. "They'll cut you some slack."

"Maybe," he said, and she saw the corner of his mouth twitch. "But they tend to think it's your fault no matter what. Even if you weren't anywhere around when it happened."

"I'm just glad we both walked away," she said softly.

"Me, too," he agreed, and reached over to take her hand in his. It was a casual, unstudied move that seemed utterly natural, and even now Alex was a little surprised at how right it felt.

"I hope you're not in trouble with your boss," she said.

"Lawrence? No, he's all right. He's sort of…used to odd things from me."

She knew Justin had taken his share of heat for his involvement in the entire Athena investigation last year. But he'd never talked about it, so she'd assumed he worked it out with his superiors, as she had with hers. Of course, the spectacular results had been very hard to argue with, even with the brass.

"He's been around this business long enough to have a few unresolved things of his own hanging heavy over his head," he went on, "so he understands the need to tackle cold cases."

"But this one's not even yours."

"It's the bureau's," he said. "That's good enough for him."

Relieved, she leaned back in the seat. Between the

adrenaline rush and resultant crash, the hours of explaining and giving official statements, and the lack of sleep from the night before, Alex knew she was running low on reserves. Knew that was when she was sometimes less than tactful. So she picked her next words carefully.

"Your office, this is really their jurisdiction. Do you think they'll get in our way?"

"On the Gracelyn case? I don't think so. Not yet, anyway. Their first concern will be who tried to blow up two of their agents, I think." He gave her a sideways look. "How's your boss going to react?"

Alex sighed. "I don't think she'll be surprised. Not after last year."

He grinned at her. "Just a couple of problem children, aren't we?"

"That'd be us," she said, smiling in spite of her weariness.

"So," he said, as casually as if he were still joking, "whose toes do you think we stepped on?"

"Somebody's," she agreed. "And hard, for them to risk killing two federal agents."

"Indeed," he said, and she caught a trace of an undercurrent in his voice. He was, she realized suddenly, angry. On the surface he was joking and bucking her up, but underneath...

As they pulled up to a stoplight she asked, "Which part are you angrier about? That they blew up your car, or that nobody saw anything?"

The canvas of the area around the restaurant had turned up nothing. Neither had a check of his neighborhood; no one had seen anyone loitering around his apartment or the parking garages.

"What I'm angry about," he said, not bothering to even try to deny the emotion, "is that whoever planted that thing got close enough to do it. It means I was asleep at the wheel."

"Then both of us were," she pointed out. "But I don't think so. I think they just planted it while we were in the restaurant."

"Then they had to have followed us there."

"Did they?"

"How else?"

"The maître d' called you by name."

He looked at her, brow furrowed. She shrugged. He'd get there, she knew. And he did, just as the light changed and they began to move again.

"Are you saying they knew I go there? That they've been watching me?"

"I'm just saying you're the local. I'm not, not anymore. You're the one who has established habits here that could be noticed. Or perhaps found out."

He clearly didn't like the idea, but after a moment he let out a compressed breath and said, "Damn. You're right." He slid her a sideways glance as they turned into his apartment building. "You should be a field agent."

"No, thanks. I'll stick to trace evidence, thank you. People are too darned irrational."

He gave a wry laugh. "I won't argue with that." He turned the engine off and sat back in the seat. "I haven't worked anything out of this office that would have made me wary about being tracked."

"Oh, I'm sure it's our poking around that brought it on," she said.

"So they used me to find us and make a move."

He sounded so disgusted she felt an unaccustomed urge to comfort. "We knew we'd be stirring things up, but neither one of us knew we were poking a live rattler's nest," she pointed out.

There was a pause in their assessment as they got out of the borrowed car and did a thorough recon of the garage, and inside it her parked rental car. Then they inspected the area around his apartment, and did an even more thorough inspection of the apartment itself, inside and out. Agents and local police had already been there, but nobody had as much at stake as they did, so they did it all again themselves.

They found nothing the others had missed, and headed inside at last.

"So, what does all this tell us?" he asked as they finally closed and locked the door.

Alex dropped her purse on the tan leather sofa and kicked off her shoes gratefully. The apartment was delightfully cool, and she wondered if the fact that they were in the desert and it looked like desert made her feel it was hot even when the weather was spring-time mild as it was now.

"One," she said, answering him as she unclipped her weapon and dropped it on the sofa beside her purse, "is that it is a rattler's nest. Two, that they're already scared."

Justin stretched expansively. "Three, they've got a lot to lose, to risk the FBI coming down on them full force."

"So…we shuffle everything and put those with the most to lose at the top."

"Problem is figuring out who that is. I mean, what's important to them might not seem that important to us."

Alex sighed. "Like I said, irrational."

"People get that way when they're scared of losing something precious to them." He yawned.

"They also get that way when they're exhausted," Alex said.

"Point taken. Shall we pick this up in the morning?"

"I hate to break it to you, but it's been morning for hours now."

"Well then," he said, stepping over to her and beginning a gentle massage of her shoulders that made her knees threaten to give out, "we're behind."

"Mmm," she murmured, suddenly all she could manage to say.

"Sleep first," Justin said softly. "And then we'll… attend to other things."

She didn't even remember hitting the pillow.

She did remember, with erotic clarity, when she'd

awakened with Justin caressing her, sending her halfway to the top before she even had her eyes open. And then he'd slid into her and sent her the rest of the way, the sound of him shouting her name echoing in her ears.

"I'm beginning to see a pattern here," Alex said.

"Me, too," Justin agreed. "What's yours?"

"That nearly everybody at the top of my list is back in D.C."

"Yeah, I noticed that."

"What was yours?"

"Actually, a lack of a pattern. I can't see any correlation between repeated contacts and those bank withdrawals. Or her appointments. And she had just made one of those withdrawals three days before she was killed."

Alex leaned back in his kitchen chair. "Meaning?"

"If she was being blackmailed, I'm not sure it had anything to do with her murder."

"She was paying, so why would they kill the golden goose?"

"Exactly."

She couldn't deny the logic there. "I don't know that it has anything to do with this silly spider thing, either," she said. She gestured at the stack of e-mails they'd pulled off Christine's computer.

"What did you find?" Justin asked.

"There's a couple in here from somebody calling

themselves only 'A,' and talking about spinning webs all over the world. I would have written it off as some spam about the Internet, World Wide Web and all that, if Marion hadn't saved it."

"What's your feel?"

"I've got no evidence except my gut," Alex said, "but I think this spider thing is something separate. Important but separate."

"Your gut's good enough for me," he said. "Let me see your list."

Gratified by his easy acceptance, she shoved the notepad over to him, curious to see what his reaction would be to the list of names. She'd pulled them out of the senatorial files, selecting people Marion had clashed with: people who didn't agree with her philosophy and took it personally that she was so successful at spreading it; people whose expensive pet and pork-barrel projects she had shot down with vigor; people she had embarrassed by publicly exposing the flawed logic or outright deception in their positions.

It was a long list.

His reaction was a long, low whistle.

"Wow. This is some group of famous names."

"Famous in some circles, infamous in others."

"Talk about the echelons of power. You're really going to stir up trouble if you go poking around these names."

"I already have, judging by the condition of your car," she said.

His mouth curved into a wry grimace. "Good point. So…what are you going to do?"

"Go back to where I started from, I guess."

"Back to D.C."

She nodded. "Got a copy of *Don Quixote* around? I need to read up on tilting at windmills."

Chapter 14

Alex sat up in her own bed in the Alexandria house, achingly aware of how empty it was. And a little surprised at how quickly she had gotten used to Justin being with her. Not just for sex—not that it hadn't gotten anything but better—but during the night, when she could feel his warmth, and in the morning.

She missed having him right here to talk to first thing, and that surprised her even more. She'd thought she was perfectly content alone. And perhaps she had been, but she was beginning to think it might have been because she didn't know any different.

A sad state of affairs at her age, she thought, but

she was smiling, knowing that state was gone now, blasted to pieces by her very own Dark Angel.

As if on cue, the phone rang. Justin had been so strongly in her mind she half expected it to be him, but it was her grandfather.

"Good morning, dear. Sleep well?"

Actually, no, she thought, but decided against saying so and having to explain why. While she was savoring the changes in her life, she didn't quite feel ready to discuss them yet, not even with her beloved G.C.

They exchanged a few more niceties before he asked, "How did things go in Phoenix?"

She knew better than to lie to him, and she hadn't forgotten the recent lesson he'd taught her about protecting him. "We had a little trouble, but we gathered a lot of information."

G.C. chuckled. "A little trouble? My, but that's a tactful way to put it."

So he did already know. She'd suspected as much. The man had sources and contacts around the globe. And he was remarkably calm about such things.

And now he was chuckling, so he wasn't going to come down hard on her. Not that he ever did, even when she had it coming.

"I've got a list of names I'd like to go over with you," she told him. "Do you have some time?"

"Of course."

That had been the answer she'd gotten her entire life, even well before she'd had the slightest idea how busy and prominent a man her grandfather was. He ever and always had had time for her, and she'd been stunned to learn later on in her life that he'd once put a prime minister on hold for her.

"I love you, G.C.," she said suddenly, unable to hold it back even if she'd wanted to.

"I know," he said, and somehow that was a much better answer than just an expressed return of the emotion.

She was dressing when the phone rang again. This time it was Justin.

"It's too quiet here," he said.

"Here, too," she said. "And empty."

"Oh, yeah."

His voice had gone low and husky, as if he knew she'd been referring to her bed. As he probably had. She was learning not to underestimate him.

After a moment he cleared his throat and said, "I finally got the dump on that pay-as-you-go cell phone. You got it right, I think."

"Got what right?"

"Most of the calls on it are to D.C.—unlisted numbers. So that's going to take a while, but your boy was definitely calling somebody there."

He gave her the list of numbers and she added them to her ever-expanding stack of notes and papers and pages upon pages of reports. Allison had sent copies of everything she had found of her mother's, which added a good inch to the stack of personal papers, which Alex hadn't had a chance to go through completely yet.

"Got the ballistics on his handgun, too," Justin said.

"Let me guess," Alex said wearily. "It doesn't match anything in any database."

"Gee, how'd you guess?" His tone was nearly as wry as hers, and that made her smile.

After that, saying goodbye was suddenly awkward. Sex had definitely changed the dynamic. But she told him she was on her way to the farm, and he said to say hello to G.C. for him, and it was finally done.

Odd, she thought as she drove. It had never been so hard before. Perhaps it was all part of this moving to a new stage.

By noon she was at the farm, and after a rocketing run over the cross-country course aboard Twill, she was ready to tackle the mass of data and names.

First, across the simple lunch Sylvia had placed on the table set up on the big, farmhouse-style porch outside, she handed G.C. the list.

"I'm looking for any names to take off the list, or any to move higher up."

She made no further comment, merely watched him for reaction to any of the names. She was aware that he knew many of them. Wouldn't be surprised to find he knew them all. But she wanted his first, gut reaction, uncolored by her own suspicions.

She saw his eyes pause a time or two, and once she saw surprise, but G.C. had a finely honed poker face, and she doubted anyone who didn't know him as well as she did would be able to read him at all.

"Well," he said as he finally set down the page and nudged it back toward her. "That's quite a list."

"I know."

"When you stir up the pot, you don't do it halfway, do you?"

She smiled sweetly at him. "Wonder where I learned that?"

He chuckled, then gestured at the list. "Take off Rafski and Porter."

He didn't explain why, and she didn't ask; Charles Bennington Forsythe hadn't arrived at this position in life by being stupid or easily fooled.

"All right," she said, and put a line through both names with the red pen she'd brought out for the purpose.

"I'd move Eckman and Yates and Duran down on the list. I don't care for them personally, but I don't think they'd resort to murder."

She noticed he wasn't asking her why any of these names were on the list. Either he already knew, which wouldn't surprise her, or he trusted her as she trusted him. That made her smile inwardly as she marked those names with blue.

He said nothing after that for a long moment. Alex just waited, knowing that G.C. wouldn't add his weight to her suspicions without long and careful thought.

"Rollins could move up," he said finally. "And

perhaps Corbin. They're ruthless enough. And Rankin was next in line for Marion's committee seat on Ways and Means."

"That's a big feather, isn't it?"

"One of the biggest. And Rankin wasn't happy when she got it."

She circled the two names. And waited again. The silence drew out.

"I'm not going to mention him," G.C. finally said. "You know I can't be fair about him. We've been adversaries too long."

She knew who he meant. He was way down on the list simply because of the unlikeliness of it. His name had been part of the folklore of her childhood, back when she'd thought of him simply as "The Enemy."

Anybody who disagreed with her grandfather was, of course, wrong, but anybody who resorted to calling him names and then later telling lies was the personification of what she'd come to hate about this town.

"Don't worry," she said. "I'll do that part."

"Let Justin do it," G.C. suggested, to her surprise. "He won't have the prejudice we do."

She stared at him for a moment. Her wonder that he'd suggested Justin was quickly overtaken by her admiration for this man who was her grandfather.

"He's given you little but grief, unfairly castigated you in public forums, linked your name to a string of people he's endlessly lambasted in the press, barely stopped short of false accusations, and you're worried about being fair to him?"

G.C. smiled. "Don't you see? Those are the very reasons I—we—must take the high road. He's incapable of it."

Her chest tightened with emotion, seeming to squeeze at her heart. She reached across the table and took his hand in hers.

"Charles Bennington Forsythe, you are truly an amazing man," she said softly. "If time travel were possible, Washington and Jefferson would be proud to have you to dinner."

G.C. laughed. "Now there's a sizable compliment! Thank you, my dear girl. I only hope I can continue to be the man you think I am."

He squeezed her hand, and for a moment neither of them spoke or needed to. Finally he released his grasp and turned back to the task at hand.

"Now. What else can I do to help? If you want to see these people, do you need me to make some calls?"

She'd been thinking about this. "Not yet. I think I'd like to nibble around the edges a bit first. Like with the people who would know them best but not feel compelled to tell them someone's asking questions?"

"Hmm." He looked thoughtful. "You could talk to Marlene, Corbin's housekeeper, I suppose."

Alex thought a moment, then placed the woman. She worked for the man who had inherited a business empire, without, some said, the acumen to run it.

"The one whose oldest daughter I taught to ride years back?"

He nodded. "I'm sure she's still grateful enough to help you. And talk to our Jacob right now. He's close with Senator Rankin's valet."

"All right."

Alex couldn't quite get past someone still using the word *valet* in a context that didn't include car keys at the restaurant. But Rankin was old school, and that was the least of his affectations. It would be interesting to see what Jacob Garner, who had been the Forsythe's head groom most of her life, had to say.

She started by saying, "I won't lie to you, Jacob, this is not just personal. I don't want you to find out later and think I pumped you without telling you why."

"And that is why I will answer you as best I can," he answered.

What the wiry man had to say, after some prodding and insistence that she wanted the truth, not pap cleaned up for her consumption, was telling if not helpful. Gerard, Rankin's valet, was nearly as self-absorbed as his employer. He had apparently bought in to Rankin's opinion of his own importance, ergo the idea that this made *him* more important.

Once she got Jacob talking, Alex picked up a brush and began to help with the grooming of the young bay he was working on. It was something she liked doing, and it would do the filly good to get used to more than one person working on her.

"He doesn't socialize with the likes of me," Jacob said. "Or anyone else who works for anyone he considers 'lesser' than 'the senator.'"

"Does he talk about Rankin?"

"Endlessly," Jacob said with a roll of his eyes.

Alex chuckled. "That bad?" she asked as she worked the red-brown coat to a high shine.

"Worse. To hear him tell it, you'd think the man had more power than the president."

"Does he ever say anything about Rankin personally? Like does the senator rant, go off on anyone, threaten anyone?"

Jacob's dark eyes widened, as if he'd only now recalled that Alex worked for the FBI. But he answered. "He calls people names. Anybody who doesn't agree with him or his mentor, the grand Waterton, is an idiot and doesn't deserve to live."

"Typical partisan stuff, then," Alex said.

"Sad to say," Jacob agreed.

"Did you ever get the feeling Gerard thought he would actually do something…extreme to any of those opposition people?"

"Extreme?"

Jacob looked puzzled, but Alex knew it was likely because it would never occur to him that people might actually do violence when their views were challenged. She waited, and saw understanding dawn gradually.

"You mean…hurt someone?"

"Or worse."

The man let out a low whistle. "I can't say for sure, but Gerard once said, as if he were proud of it, that his boss could be as ruthless as he had to be."

Did that include murder? Would the man actually murder another United States senator for political reasons?

"I don't much like you having to deal with this kind of thing, Miss Alex," Jacob said.

"Sometimes neither do I," she admitted.

"Jacob deserves a raise," Alex told her grandfather when she returned to the house.

"Do you know what I'm paying him?" G.C. asked.

"No, but whatever it is, he deserves more."

G.C. laughed. "Yes, he does, dear. But he won't take it."

Alex blinked. "What?"

"I tried to give him a raise at the first of the year. He told me he was already making nearly double that of his colleagues in similar positions, and that was quite sufficient, thank you."

Alex laughed. "That sounds like him, all right."

"Was he of any help?"

"In specifics, no. Adding to the database, yes. And he told me enough to know talking to Rankin's man would be a waste of time."

"That helps. What's next?"

She sighed. "I don't know. I need to talk to other people, Rankin's friends, and Whitman, our favorite lobbyist, and a couple of others. But I don't want to tip them off by asking anyone directly."

"Well, my dear," her grandfather said, "there's only one easy way I can think of to pump the people around them."

"And that is?"

"Doing what you least like to do."

Her brow furrowed as she looked at him. And then, when she saw the teasing twinkle in his eyes, she groaned.

"Oh, Lord, no. Not that. Anything but that."

"Face it, girl, it's the best way. The least likely to arouse suspicions. And they'll be so startled, they won't even think about your motive."

He was right. Damn it, Alex thought, he was right. It was the best, easiest, least obtrusive way to get information on some of the stellar lights of beltway society.

Alex Forsythe, FBI agent and forensic scientist, was going to become Alexandra Catherine Forsythe, former debutante and society belle.

"I'll warn your mother," G.C. said, and Alex thought it uncharacteristically cruel of him to laugh about it.

Chapter 15

"Why, Veronica, I had no idea your daughter was back in town! I had the idea she was off in Myanmar, or some such exotic place."

Alex bit her lip and managed to keep from pointing out to Mrs. Elizabeth Garfield that officially it was still Burma to the United States. She also managed to keep herself from flicking a glance at her mother, who no doubt had spread the exotic-place tale herself, to avoid embarrassment over the fact that they barely spoke.

"Oh, I've been all over," Alex said, affecting the breezy, superficial tone she heard all too much of at these gatherings. That much, at least, hadn't changed since she'd sworn them off years ago, the moment she turned twenty-one and could say no to her mother without feeling as if she was sassing her. "But there's no place like home, is there?"

The woman smiled, clearly without a clue that Alex hadn't meant it as a compliment. She still thought of the farm, and not D.C. and Alexandria and this crowd as home.

G.C. had been right, of course. She'd realized the moment she thought about it that to get this done, she was going to have to resort to something she rarely used, something she had spent most of her life refusing to trade on.

Her name.

The Forsythe name was a point of pride to her, showing that she belonged to G.C. and the line of ancestors who had helped build this country, who in less than four centuries had made it more powerful, wealthy and strong than many civilizations that had been around for thousands of years, so much so that it could generously help less fortunate neighbors.

It was a point of pride to her mother because—and sometimes Alex thought only because—it bought her access to gatherings like this, which was being held at one of the most exclusive country clubs in the entire country. You had to be sponsored by an active member and seconded by three other members to even be considered for membership.

"You look wonderful, dear," Mrs. Garfield assured

her, as if Alex had asked. "I'd quite forgotten how lovely you are. Who did your dress?"

It was a sleek, silver-blue column of satin knit that even Alex had to admit did wonders for her figure and made her blue eyes pop.

She also had to admit she had one person to thank for it.

"Actually," Alex said, figuring she owed the sop for the help, "it's Mother's. Isn't it exquisite?"

Veronica Forsythe blushed with practiced ease. "Thank you, Alexandra. I do think it's so much fun that we can share clothes."

"And a tribute to you," Alex said. It was only half syrup; she knew her mother worked hard at staying fit and trim, and Alex knew what a battle that could be.

Clearly quite pleased with her newly sociable daughter, Veronica took Alex's arm and began to lead her around the crowded reception room, reintroducing her to people Alex hadn't seen in years. Anyone who read the gossip columns, or looked at the high-society photos, would recognize the names and faces.

Alex did neither, in fact had worked hard to put this side of her world out of her life. Except for the occasion when G.C. would ask her to hostess a small party for him—G.C., thankfully, never threw soirees like this one—she rarely even thought about this aspect of the world she'd left behind.

The shoes, she thought as she flexed feet that

weren't used to three-inch heels for long hours anymore. That's what I'd really like to leave behind.

She told herself to quit whining and pretend she was working undercover. Then she saw her mother was zeroing in on Clarice Pennington, and she forgot all about her feet. This was one of the reasons she was here, and she snapped back to full attention on the task at hand.

"Clarice!" her mother exclaimed. "You remember my daughter, Alexandra?"

Alex plastered her best—she'd been practicing the long-lost art—social smile on her face. It was a fine line between welcoming and gushing, and she hadn't walked it in a long time. But it seemed to work, for with a little effort she was able to get Clarice talking enough to steer the conversation the way she wanted.

Of course, the fact that Clarice was always glad to remind people of her marriage to a powerful politician didn't hurt. The fact that, according to his beaming wife, said husband was about to happily retire to join the board of directors of an international corporation—a job that would likely pay him much more than his current public service—bumped him down on her list.

As her mother and their hostess diverged into a discussion of new applicants for the country club, she managed to extricate herself. She wandered a bit, waving as if she were delighted to be here, yet never stopping long enough to get sucked into conversations she was certain were similar to the one she'd just escaped.

"Alex?"

The female voice from behind her tickled something in her memory, and she turned around. She stared at the pretty brunette for a moment before it came back to her.

"Pepper?"

"I thought that was you! What are you doing here? I thought you swore off these things forever."

For the first time tonight Alex was able to greet someone with genuine happiness. During her childhood, Alex had been as close to Patricia Anderson—nicknamed Pepper after her sadly unimaginative choice of Salt as a name for her white horse—as to anyone before she'd gone to Athena. They had shared a distaste for—and probably fear of—the world they would be expected to be part of when they grew up.

But when the time had come, Pepper had taken to it like Charm had taken to the desert, while Alex felt going to Athena had rescued her. They'd gone their own ways since, and lost touch except for the annual Christmas-card-guilt confession. Alex had wondered about her now and then, sadly contemplating the very real possibility that Pepper had been eaten up by that world and had become a carbon copy of her socialite mother.

"It's been so long," Pepper said. "And I know I've been awful about—"

She stopped when Alex held up a hand. "That road runs both ways. Shall we admit we've both been bad about keeping in touch and go from there? It will save a lot of time and excuses."

Pepper laughed. "That's what I always loved about you, Alex. Cut right to the chase."

She didn't seem at all offended, and Alex didn't miss the impish glint in her warm-brown eyes. Perhaps there was some of her childhood friend left here after all.

"Let's go hide and catch up," Pepper said, grabbing Alex's hand and tugging her toward the French doors that led out onto a terrace that had ever and always been graced with far too much cherub statuary for Alex's comfort. But she went, and they found a curved stone bench to sit on, in the shadow of a wisteria tree in wild bloom, dripping with so many lilac-colored flowers it didn't seem possible it was real.

It didn't take more than a few minutes of Pepper's chattering—and for all her sins, she spent little time on herself, being quite happy with her life—for Alex to realize she had an invaluable resource here. She felt a little qualm at pumping her old friend for information, but if she was going to run on and on anyway...

"—and Chad's wife is pregnant again," Pepper was saying as Alex tuned back in.

"Isn't that about number five?" Alex asked.

"Four," Pepper said with a barely concealed shudder. "Can you imagine?"

"I'd rather not," Alex said, having grown up with a mother unable to deal with only two. "But Maria is so good with them, she'll probably do fine. Some women have the knack."

While she was speaking, she was trying to think of a way to guide the conversation to where she needed it to go. But Pepper was on a gossip roll. Alex tried to pay enough attention to keep her going until she could steer her toward the people she needed to know about.

Across the terrace, Alex saw a familiar figure. Senator Eldon Waterton, from his reputation no doubt returning from some assignation in the bushes, Alex thought wryly, half expecting some disheveled young thing to emerge from the same direction.

She wondered if it would be considered cynicism if it was true.

Pepper saw him, too, apparently, because she whispered, "Have you heard about Pierre and Charlene?"

Charlene was the youngest daughter of the senator, who was now glancing their way. She saw him frown, or perhaps it was just a squint as he peered at them, then hurried on.

Alex doubted he was worried; no one seemed to care much anymore about his peccadilloes. Perhaps because they seemed so ludicrous these days—a man his age cavorting with twenty-somethings. Or perhaps simple longevity and endurance—and notoriety and fame—earned you immunity in his world.

"No. What?" she asked, turning her attention back to Pepper.

"Charlene's in town to get away, because he's been having this very blatant affair with, of all people, her hair stylist," Pepper said. "Everybody knew except Charlene. So now they're divorcing, although you'd think Charlene would have learned from her mother how to just live with it."

"Perhaps she learned from her that she didn't want to," Alex suggested.

"Maybe. But anyway, they hired the two most cut-throat attorneys back in Phoenix. Mom says by the time the lawyers are done there won't be any money left to fight over, it'll all be in the lawyer's pockets."

"That's one way to resolve a financial dispute," Alex said. The Watertons were notoriously wealthy, and Charlene had come into a huge trust fund when she'd turned twenty-one. She'd begun wildly spending, and had met the handsome, charming Pierre Laroque shortly thereafter. Despite everyone's suspicions that he had his eyes on said trust fund as much as on the pretty but spoiled Charlene, she'd married him a year later.

Alex was beginning to see the point of trusts set up so that the beneficiary couldn't touch them until they were older. If her grandfather had done that, maybe there would be more left of her brother Ben's.

Maybe if he hadn't been able to get to it until he was fifty, she thought, then felt guilty, as she always did when she thought that way about her exasperating but much beloved brother.

Trust Tory, she told herself yet again. She says there's more going on with Ben than you know, so believe it.

"They have a daughter, don't they?" Alex asked.

"Yes, and she's devastated. Charlene's dad is furious," Pepper answered.

"I'll bet," Alex said. Waterton was notoriously short-tempered, and his tippling habit didn't help matters any.

"Have you seen Rich Corbin lately?" Alex asked, hoping to use the mention of another acquaintance from their age group to nudge Pepper around to Richard Corbin senior, a name near the top of her list.

"Oh, he's in Japan," Pepper said. "He's running the Asian branch of the company."

Alex spotted her opening. "They must be doing well, then. Last I heard the Asian office was only a glimmer in his father's eyes."

"Oh, yes. His dad got some legal thing out of the way a few years ago and they've been booming."

…got some legal thing out of the way.

Alex's breath caught.

"Did he say that? That he 'got it out of the way'?"

"Something like that," Pepper said, frowning in puzzlement, no doubt at Alex's interest in the specific wording. "But honestly, it was years ago, I don't really remember."

Alex did. She knew exactly what that legal thing was.

Marion Gracelyn.

Alex's mind raced as she tried to remember. She'd paid little attention to it at the time, but the basics had been in the research she'd read. Corbin had tried to stiff the military on a contract for tank armor and had gotten caught. Marion, utterly fearless and unimpressed by his wealth, had made the case a cause. It was she who had made public his now infamous memo saying that "It doesn't matter, it's just the Army."

He'd been stunned by the outcry, and had to step down as CEO after that. Insiders knew it was merely a sop to public demand, that his replacement was mainly a figurehead and that he was still calling the shots from behind the scenes. But Alex knew he'd never forgiven Marion for his public humiliation. That she'd only exposed his genuine attitude to the world was beside the point; it was still, in his mind, her fault.

But his company had recovered. Some suggested he'd bought its way back to success, some chalked it up to the public's short memory or the fact that Corbin had some powerful politicians in his pocket.

"Alex?"

She snapped back to the conversation. "Sorry," she said quickly. "I was just thinking."

"About?"

"Oh, others that I've lost contact with. Ever see Billy Church?"

Pepper laughed. "Didn't you hear? He moved to New York with the boyfriend. Said he couldn't stand to be around his father anymore."

"As I recall, Billy's boyfriend was a heck of a lot nicer than his father is," Alex said with a grin, making Pepper laugh. Then she zeroed in on another target. "What about Bryant Rollins?"

"Oh, dear, isn't that just a mess? They've never gotten over the embarrassment of that election fraud thing. You don't see any of them anywhere anymore. I think they even dropped their club membership."

A fate worse than death, Alex thought wryly. But Bryant Sr. had been another victim of Marion Gracelyn's integrity. When he'd manipulated voter registrations and spent huge amounts of money to arrange for absentee ballots to go astray, she'd found out the truth and outed him. He'd tried to deflect it by painting her as the opposition perpetrating a smear, but by then her reputation for integrity was too established—and his too tarnished—for him to have much success.

And to add insult to injury, he lost anyway, by a margin big enough to make his efforts irrelevant.

I'll bet that's what bothered him the most, Alex guessed. Bryant Rollins Sr. was not the kind of man who would ever accept being irrelevant. And she could easily see him being out for revenge.

"What are *you* up to?" Pepper asked. "You're still with the FBI, right? Doing that CSI thing? Is it as exciting as it is on TV?"

"Hardly," she said, although she supposed having a car blow up almost underneath you might qualify as excitement in some people's view. "Most of our excitement happens in the lab."

Pepper wrinkled her nose; science had never been a favorite subject of hers. "Well, someone has to do it, I guess. And you were always good at it. You were always good at everything. So, have you found a man who appreciates you yet?"

An image of Justin popped into her head with a vividness that nearly made her gasp.

"Well, well," Pepper said. "I think I'll take that expression as a yes. Do tell!"

Alex answered with as little as she thought she could get away with. Her relationship with Justin, and its changed parameters, was something that was still too new to chat about carelessly.

As early as she could without insulting anyone, including her mother, Alex slipped away from the party. It was a warm spring night, and she gratefully kicked off the strappy high-heeled sandals once she was outside. And nearly groaned aloud at the relief as she walked normally down to the portico where the parking attendant stand was.

"Ready for your car?" The young, red-jacketed valet was earnest and exceedingly polite, managing not to laugh at her in a floor-length gown with bare toes sticking out and a pair of spike-heeled shoes in her hand.

She smiled at him for that. He blushed.

"Yes, thank you," she told him.

"I'll be right back, Ms. Forsythe."

He was good, too, she thought, if he remembered her name out of the hundred or so people there.

He was also, she thought after a few minutes, incredibly slow. The parking lot wasn't that big, even if you included the overflow lot down the hill a few yards. Yet she hadn't even heard—

Ah, she thought as she heard an engine start from the back of the lot, there it is.

Her mood changed yet again as she heard the squeal of tires.

Leave ten thousand miles of wear on the asphalt, why don't you? she muttered inwardly.

She saw the top of her small SUV over the roofs of the shorter cars in the lot as it careened her way. And there was literally no other way to describe the racing, skidding approach. He nearly clipped the corner of the big limo parked at the closest end of the row.

Her annoyance grew.

The valet had seemed nice, she thought, but this was ridiculous.

He made the last turn and headed toward her, still speeding.

She noticed three things at once.

The driver no longer had on the red jacket.

He was accelerating.

Right toward her.

No time to think. Her car leaped up over the curb, came after her like a hungry tiger. The driver seemed to realize he was in trouble. Tried to swerve. She knew there wasn't enough room.

Alex dove right. Behind the concrete pillar that held up the portico. Rolled. Prayed it would hold. Not sure it could.

A split second later, still bearing down on her, her car plowed into the pillar.

The pillar held.

It cracked. Leaned. Chunks fell.

But it held.

Alex rolled to her feet, heedless of the damage already done to her mother's hideously expensive dress. Her ears were ringing from the explosive, grinding sound of the impact. Despite that, she heard a faint tinkling sound. Realized it was bits of glass falling from the shattered windshield.

Something had clipped her left arm. She felt the sting and the wetness of blood. Instinctively she flexed it, assessed. Not impaired, she quickly decided.

She couldn't see into the crumpled car from where

Chapter 16

The pillar held.

It cracked. Leaned. Chunks fell.

But it held.

Alex rolled to her feet, heedless of the damage already done to her mother's hideously expensive dress. Her ears were ringing from the explosive, grinding sound of the impact. Despite that, she heard a faint tinkling sound. Realized it was bits of glass falling from the shattered windshield.

Something had clipped her left arm. She felt the sting and the wetness of blood. Instinctively she flexed it, assessed. Not impaired, she quickly decided.

She couldn't see into the crumpled car from where

she was, but she could see movement in the driver's seat. He was alive.

She stepped forward, toward the car, ignoring the stabs at the soles of her bare feet as she encountered debris from the wreckage.

The driver trying to extricate himself wasn't the parking valet, but she'd expected that. She hoped the young man was still alive.

Then she focused completely on the matter at hand.

The driver and car thief, someone she didn't recognize, had gotten himself almost out of the car. But he'd had to stop to try to free his right foot from some entanglement. That gave her the precious seconds she needed.

As he twisted to shove at something in the damage cab, she moved swiftly. Came up behind him. Jammed the object in her hand into his back.

"Don't move. FBI."

He went still as commanded. The FBI announcement didn't surprise him, she noted. She could almost feel him assessing, and she wondered if he was trying to figure out where in the slinky dress she'd hidden the gun jammed into his back.

"Who sent you?"

"Don't know what the hell you're talking about, lady. Ouch!"

This as she shoved harder into his back. "You just totaled my car. I *liked* that car. Talk."

"No way."

He looked like a cousin to the man in the desert, she thought. Whoever was behind this, he should work on his hiring practices. He needed to get better quality in his work force.

"When he hired you, didn't he give you a story to tell if you got caught?"

"Yeah, but—" He broke off, realizing he'd been suckered.

She knew she didn't have much more time. She exerted a little more pressure with her right hand, digging into his flesh. "Tell me who sent you, and I won't shoot you and pretend I had to do it to keep you from hitting me."

He swore, a string of words she hadn't heard in a while. "You won't. You can't. He told me you're a cop, you'd have to explain."

So he had known who—or at least what—she was. "I'll lie," she said sweetly. "Not hard to do when someone's trying to kill you."

"Son of a bitch, he said you'd be easy," the man muttered. "Said you were just some lab rat."

I'm also part of Athena Force, she told him silently. We're *never* easy.

She heard the commotion behind them, and knew the crash had been heard inside and they were about to draw a crowd. With a sigh she gave up the threat tactic.

"He was wrong. But then he usually is, didn't you know that?"

The man twisted his head to give her a sideways

glare from muddy-brown eyes that were bloodshot. Hung over? she wondered. Or worse?

"Don't know anything about him," he muttered. "Except he wants you dead. Bad."

"That," Alex said grimly, "I already figured out."

The crowd drawn from the party arrived, the clamor growing as they saw what had happened. Soon they were surrounded by onlookers and, thankfully, the security guard for the club.

"Could somebody call 911?" Alex asked. Then, with some relish, she moved her right hand and stepped back, letting the driver see her "gun."

"Before my shoe goes off," she added, brandishing the spike heel in his face, and grinning at the man's stupefied expression.

"That's his story and he's sticking to it," Alex told G.C. wearily.

They were at the farm, having breakfast on the back porch overlooking the fields. When she'd called last night, knowing he'd hear it from someone and wanting it to be her first, G.C. had insisted she come and stay until this was resolved. Since she much preferred it to the house in Alexandria anyway, she'd acquiesced.

Not that the Alexandria place wasn't a lovely house, but Alex was a country girl who loved the green, rolling hills of the Virginia horse country and, much to her mother's dismay, would rather muck out a stall than take tea on the patio.

G.C. took another sip of his morning coffee, and Alex took a bite of Sylvia Barrett's delicious omelet, feeling only a faint twinge from the cut on her bandaged arm, before they returned to her tale of last night's events.

"But he admitted to you someone had sent him?" G.C. asked.

"Not in so many words, but yes, he did. He referred to a 'he' who told him what to do. But I guess he figures better to take a fall for battery than attempted murder, so to the cops he's insisting he just stole the car and lost control because he didn't know how to drive it. That he had no idea who it belonged to, that he just took mine because that was the one the valet had unlocked and had the keys to."

"How is the valet?"

"I called the hospital first thing this morning. He's going to be okay. The guy slugged him pretty good, and he needed a few stitches, but no permanent damage."

"Good. I hope you asked them to let us know if he needs anything?"

She nodded. "I feel bad for him, he just got in the way of…whatever this is."

"What it is," G.C. said sternly, "is a big mistake. And when we find out who's behind it, they will be eternally sorry."

For some reason this seemed like the opening she'd always been waiting for.

"G.C.? Just how well did you know Marion Gracelyn?"

"Why, she was a family friend for years. You know that."

He wasn't looking at her. G.C. never avoided looking at her when he spoke to her.

"I didn't mean the family," Alex said softly. "I meant you."

His gaze snapped to her face. For the first time in her life Alex saw her grandfather involuntarily betray surprise.

And she guessed she had her answer.

"Alex, there was never anything untoward—"

He stopped when she shook her head. "Of course there wasn't, G.C. You wouldn't. And I don't think she would have. But wow."

"Wow?"

"Talk about the dynamic duo. The mind boggles to think what a powerhouse that would have created. Definite wow."

To her relief he smiled. "Thank you, my dear."

He didn't say for what, but Alex knew. "I'd never judge you, Grandpa. You never judge me, after all."

Her use of the more common appellation made his eyebrows rise, but he only smiled at her. And then changed the subject.

"What exactly did you do at this party, my girl, to so rile things up?"

Alex, who had already weathered the storm of her

mother's hysteria—centered on the damaged dress after she discovered Alex was for the most part un-hurt—needed her grandfather's calm assessment just now. So, quickly she told him what she'd learned tonight. All of it. Although, she wasn't sure some of it was relevant. Any of it, for that matter.

"It could all be just the usual gossip making the rounds," she said when she finished.

"It could," her grandfather agreed. "It's fairly typical, I'm afraid."

Alex heard the chirp coming from inside the house, from the intercom that signaled someone at the gate. She glanced at her grandfather, who shook his head and said, "Sylvia will get it."

"Expecting someone?"

"Yes," he said. "Someone helpful. Now then, where were we?"

"Gossip," Alex said, wondering who would be coming out here at this early hour, helpful or otherwise.

"Ah. I can at least tell you that the references to Marion are accurate, on the surface at least. She did expose Corbin's putting our troops at risk, and Collin's fraudulent voting plan. It was quite the buzz at the time, both times."

"Do you know how angry they really were?"

"Quite. Angry enough to kill? I don't know."

"She wasn't killed until a couple of years after," Alex pointed out. "Three years, in Corbin's case."

"A long time for the heat of passion to cool."

"Do either of them have the mind-set to act that coldly, so long after the fact?"

"Someone once said revenge is a fruit you must let ripen," G.C. said, leaning back in his chair, steepling his hands before him. "Do either of them have the patience to wait that long? Corbin, I'd say yes. He's had to wait a long time for his company to get back to even a semblance of what it once was. Bryant Rollins? He's—"

"—a politician. Of course he has patience."

Alex wheeled around in her wicker chair, startled. There was no mistake, as there had been no mistaking that deep, masculine voice.

Justin.

"What—" she began.

"—am I doing here, I know."

"Besides finishing everyone's sentences, that is," Alex said, her mouth quirking.

Justin grinned, walked over to stand behind her, then bent to plant a soft, tickling kiss on her ear. Involuntarily she flicked a glance at her grandfather, who seemed unmoved.

And unsurprised.

She wondered again what they'd discussed during those talks Justin had mentioned. Wondered what Justin had told G.C. to so obviously win him over.

"So? What are you doing here?" she asked. *And why can't you at least look tired, after taking what had to be a redeye flight?*

An instant later she belatedly made the connection between Justin and G.C.'s expected guest. She whirled on her grandfather.

"You called him?"

"I did," G.C. said calmly. "I thought you'd prefer him to a hired bodyguard."

"I don't need a bodyguard," she yelped. "I'm a flippin' FBI agent!"

"Yes, you are," Justin said. "But as you have pointed out, you're not a field agent."

"I'm part of Athena Force," she snapped as she shifted her attention back to Justin. "I don't need to be a field agent."

"I freely admit you're much more capable than the average scientist would be," Justin said, "but that doesn't mean you should try to handle this alone."

"You already had a narrow escape because of this," Alex said, voicing something that continued to bother her. "I don't want to be responsible for another close call. Or worse."

"That's not your call, sweetheart."

Before she could react to the unexpected endearment, her grandfather spoke.

"The waters you're stirring up aren't just muddy, Alex," he said. "They could easily turn bloody again. So just you let your old grandfather do what little he can to help you stay safe. I only made a couple of phone calls, after all."

"A couple?" Alex glared at him with as much

umbrage as she could muster, given how much she adored the man. "Justin and who else?"

"It doesn't matter," G.C. said.

"I'm here for as long as necessary," Justin said.

Alex glanced from her grandfather to Justin and back again. She'd grown up with her family's prestige and prominence and, after her grandmother's death, had played hostess for G.C. more than once. And more than one of those excursions into formal hostessing had included the president. So she was well aware of how much clout her loving grandfather had.

She also knew how his mind worked.

"So, did he call the attorney general or just go straight to the director?" she asked Justin.

Justin blinked, apparently startled. Whether at her asking him instead of her grandfather or at the question itself she couldn't tell, but it seemed he might as well find out now what he was dealing with.

Welcome to my world, she thought. Would he be able to deal with it? She hadn't thought of that. Emerson had been born to this world, but Justin had grown up far removed from anything like it.

He did, however, recover quickly. "Don't know, don't care," he said lightly. "All I know is my boss told me to get on a plane. So I did."

"So all of a sudden you're a rule-following kind of guy?" She was still a little peeved, and it rang in her voice.

"I've always been a rule-following guy," he said softly. "They're just not always *your* rules."

G.C.'s approving chuckle told her she'd been over the line. And it didn't take her long to realize that it was the idea of her grandfather and Justin in collusion about her that had her so unsettled and on edge. She wasn't sure of all the reasons why, and didn't have time to dwell on it now.

First she had to figure out who had so much to lose that they'd risk repeated attempts to murder federal agents to stop their investigation.

Chapter 17

"You ever get the feeling it's right there in front of you, if you could just see it?" Justin said glumly.

"I've felt that way for days now," Alex agreed, stopping in her pacing of the length of the porch.

She scratched absently at her arm, where the cut she'd received in the attempt at the country club was already healing and thus beginning to itch. She became aware of what she was doing and stopped. Then she turned around and went back to the table where they'd been working.

Her grandfather had left them to wrestle with things, his only advice to work out anything personal when it was over. The subtext of "and you're both still alive" wasn't spoken, but they heard it nevertheless.

"I feel like picking all this up—" he gestured at the pile of papers that had become all too familiar "—and shaking it until the answer falls out. Or maybe throw it on the floor like a deck of cards and start over in whatever order they land in."

"I know the feeling," Alex said wearily. "I'm so tired of reading the same things over and over and always coming up empty—"

She stopped herself midcomplaint. An idea was tickling around the edges of her mind. She stared at the stack of pages. Then at the lists of names: probables, possibles, unlikelies.

"Maybe," she said slowly.

"Maybe what?"

"Maybe we're going at this wrong. Maybe we're trying to force these names to fit into the puzzle. Maybe we should quit looking for who's the most likely."

He sat up straight. "You mean turn it around? Quit looking for who had the strongest motive and start looking for someone who…?"

She nodded. "We should let the puzzle pieces tell us who fits."

He grasped it immediately. "All right," he said. "Let's start with the first incident since you opened this can of worms."

"The guy who followed me to the police station

in Athens," she said. "That was the first time I was aware of anything."

"Who knew you were there?"

"At the station?"

"Let's back it up even further. Who knew you were in Phoenix at all, at any point," he said. "Who knew on your end?"

"G.C. of course. Kayla. Christine, at Athena. Eric Hunt." She slid him a sideways look. "You."

"Me," he agreed blandly. "But don't forget the others. There's hotel staff. Anybody who saw you when you were out at Athena—now, don't get yourself in an uproar, I wasn't accusing anyone, just listing—and anybody who saw you at the station."

"And anybody you talked to at your office."

"I didn't tell anyone." His mouth quirked. "I knew I'd get ragged on endlessly. They've seen you, you know."

She smiled at the implicit compliment. "Okay then, anybody at your favorite restaurant." Then she added wryly, "And if you want to get crazed, the airport, car rental agency, and—"

"Okay, slow down," he said with a laugh. "Even counting all of those people, none of them individually have anything to gain. So at most he, she or they were paid, either to report where you were or were going, or to try and stop you."

"By one person."

"In the end, yes, although there could be a chain.

At this point I think we should assume it all leads back to one person. Sometimes the easiest answer and all that."

"Okay, off the endless string for now. The first incident was the morning after I got here. Before I'd done anything except see Kayla and catch up with Christine out at Athena."

"If it was someone in Arizona, it had to be someone who could mobilize really fast."

She pondered that, turning ramifications over in her mind in view of the new focus on what had happened rather than who was behind it. What were the possibilities of someone simply spotting her as she arrived in Phoenix, and then organizing all these attempts to stop her in such a short time? Or that someone who just happened to spot her had known who to call who would be interested in what she was there to do?

"And how had they known what I was there to do in the first place?" she asked aloud. "It's not like I haven't been back to visit Athena occasionally. And last year I was coming and going all the time, with Rainy and all."

"Exactly. For them to move that fast, they almost had to already know you were coming. And why."

"But I didn't even tell Kayla and Christine why, until I got there."

Justin stayed silent for a moment before he said what had become apparent to them both. "That implies it's somebody here."

"But nobody knew here, either, except G.C. and you. Although…" Her words slowed as her thoughts shifted. "I did interview a couple of people here, before I left for Arizona. People who were against Athena in the beginning."

"People with something at stake?"

"Not obviously. General Stanley. Senator Rankin."

"Big names. Anything in their reactions?"

She shook her head. "They seemed…over it. Stanley is grudgingly neutral now. And the senator said he'd always thought it would work, he'd only opposed it for political reasons."

"Meaning he had to follow his party?"

"That's my guess."

Justin considered this. "So Rankin says he wasn't really against it, and the general was only philosophically opposed. He didn't really lose anything."

"No. No real reason for revenge, unless he's unbalanced, and I highly doubt that."

"So if it was neither of them, but we still assume it was someone here pulling the strings…" he began.

"Then maybe one of them said something to somebody else," she said. "It wouldn't take a lot to connect my questions with my trip.

"No." She thought a moment longer. "I don't think it was the general. It just doesn't feel that way."

Justin nodded in apparent agreement. "If it had been, you'd already be dead."

It took her a second to get what he meant. Then

she nodded slowly. "He'd have access to people who were a lot better at their job."

"Exactly. So who else could have ended up with both those pieces of information—that you were asking about Marion's murder and that you were heading to Arizona?"

She sighed. "It's an endless chain. Anybody could have mentioned piece A to someone who mentioned it to someone until it hit whoever had piece B."

"It must be tough, being the subject of so many conversations," Justin said. "Guess that's what happens when you're a famous Forsythe."

She lifted her gaze to look at him across the table, caught the teasing glint in his eyes. Relief washed over her. He really was joking. Maybe he would be able to handle the Forsythe world after all.

Justin, she thought, could probably handle just about anything.

She grinned at him, and had the pleasure of seeing him catch his breath in response. "Get used to it," she said.

"Oh, I will. All of it."

She decided now was not the time to dig into exactly what he meant by "all of it." If she did, they'd never make any more progress here.

Assuming they'd made any at all, of course.

"There's one more thing," she said as something else occurred to her. "Who would have reason not to believe the assumption others made, that I was writing a book about the murder."

"Someone who knew that as an active FBI agent, you'd not be likely to do that."

She nodded. "That might narrow it down a bit."

"If we can—"

The ringing of a cell phone from somewhere on the table interrupted him. It took them a moment to determine it was hers and then to locate it amid all the piles of papers.

"Alex? Kayla. I've only got a minute—I'm on my way to Athena to pick Jazz up for the weekend—but I wanted to let you know Mr. Lang sent me that list of stolen or lost cards. Do you want me to fax it or e-mail it?"

Her laptop was still packed, so she asked, "Can you fax it?"

"Sure. As soon as I get to Athena. I was going to stop and say hello to Christine anyway, so I can do it from there."

"Great. I'm at G.C.'s, so let me give you his fax number."

She rattled it off; since it was only one digit off the house number, she knew Kayla would be able to remember it without writing it down.

"Got it," Kayla said. "I'm about five minutes out, so give me ten and it's yours."

"Thanks, girlfriend. And give that girl of yours a big hug from her Auntie Alex."

Kayla laughed, but there was a touch of wistfulness in it. "She's barely a girl anymore, she's growing up so fast."

"Savor it, then," Alex said with a laugh. "The teenage horror years will be upon you before you know it."

"Oh, joy," Kayla said, but she was laughing for real when she hung up.

"What was that?" Justin asked.

Alex explained about the library computer and the card number used to make a reservation to arrange payment to the man who'd tried to jump her out in the desert behind Athena.

"You think it'll be on that list?"

"I'm not sure." She glanced at the table, her mouth quirking upward. "I just thought we needed another piece of paper."

Justin laughed. Then he grabbed her and, unexpectedly, planted a long, slow, pulse-accelerating kiss on her lips.

"So, where am I sleeping tonight?" he whispered.

"Where do you think?"

"Well, it is your grandfather's house."

"If you think G.C.'s too blind to notice things have…changed since the last time you were here, you're underestimating him."

"I would never underestimate Charles Forsythe. I just didn't know what his personal preferences were for people sleeping with his granddaughter under his roof."

"You'll have to ask him," she said. Then, wondering if he'd see the implicit compliment, she added, "The situation has never arisen before."

He looked at her steadily for a long moment. "Thank you," he finally said.

It would definitely be wise, she thought, not to underestimate Justin Cohen, either.

"Did the fax help?" G.C. asked over dinner. He'd retrieved it and brought it to them the moment it had finished printing in his office.

"Not at first glance," Alex said. "But we've compiled so many names, I want to check again against the lists."

G.C. took a bite of the fresh-grilled salmon and savored it like a man who appreciated such things before he spoke again.

"Have you spoken to your mother since last night?"

Alex sighed. "No. I just know she's going to get on my case about that dress. I understand, really, I mean it's a custom designer piece that she won't be able to replace, but—"

"You don't think she might be worried about you?" Justin asked.

She rolled her eyes. "You don't know my mother."

"Sometimes, my dear," G.C. said neutrally, "neither do you."

Alex blinked at her grandfather in surprise. This was unexpected; G.C. got along with her mother little better than she herself did.

"She was hurt that you didn't call her from Phoenix after everything that happened," G.C. said. "She does love you, Alexandra. She just doesn't show it very well. Fussing is her way. Those who like being fussed over see it that way. Those who don't…"

"All right, all right. I'll call her."

"Good."

It was later on that evening, after G.C. had bidden them good-night with a rather blatant announcement that he planned to sleep in in the morning, rather late—an announcement that made Alex blush and Justin grin—that Justin brought up her mother again.

"I understand that I barely know the woman," he said, "so I could be wrong, but your mother didn't strike me as the type who would, or could, be particularly good at keeping things to herself."

"She's not," Alex said, puzzled. "Why?"

"She knew you were going to Phoenix."

"Well, yes, of course she did. She—"

Alex stopped abruptly. She stared at Justin. Thought of her mother, and her tendency to chatter under the illusion it was charming.

Chatter. To anyone. About anything.

"My God," Alex whispered.

Did they owe the attempts on both their lives to her *mother?*

Alex dived for the telephone. Her mother was no doubt fulfilling one of her many social obligations tonight, but it was just late enough now that she might catch her on the way home.

"Hello?" Veronica Forsythe's voice was bright and cheerful, as it always was unless she was dealing with her unruly daughter.

"Mom? It's Alex."

"Alexandra, dear. How nice of you to remember my number."

Yeesh, Alex thought. "Sorry, I got a little tied up. And I meant what I told you, Mother, I'm very, very sorry about the dress. I'll get it replaced, somehow."

"Oh, don't you worry about that. It doesn't matter. I've been quite the belle of the ball, passing along the details of your adventure."

Leave it to Mom to make social hay out of attempted murder, Alex thought.

But she almost immediately chided herself; her mother had no way of knowing that's what it had been. To everyone at the gathering last night it had been presented as exactly what the suspect had said it was: a car thief who couldn't drive. Rather amusing, actually.

"So what function was it tonight?"

"Oh, the art museum fund-raiser. Just everyone was there. The Penningtons, Senator Rankin, even Secretary Dexter was there."

Alex would bet that was an interesting gathering, with Secretary of State Dexter, a lightning rod if ever there was one in Washington.

"He asked after you," Veronica said.

Alex yanked her attention back. "What? Secretary Dexter?" She'd only met the man once, for all of ten seconds.

"No, silly girl. I mean the senator. He asked how you were."

"Why on earth?"

"I suppose because he's a man who cares about family," Veronica said. "And he said it was because he couldn't quite remember what I'd said about you last week at the DAR luncheon in Arlington. He's so charming, pretending he's getting old and forgetful."

Alex went still. "He asked you specifically about me last week?"

"Well, he did after I mentioned that you were off to Phoenix."

"And again tonight?"

"Well, yes. He'd heard about your little incident at the country club, so of course he wanted to know if you were all right."

I'll just bet he did, Alex thought with an inward grimace.

She didn't remember much more of the conversation. She must have made some sense, because her mother seemed perfectly amiable by the time they hung up.

"Alex? What's wrong? What did she say?"

"She told a crowd at a luncheon last week that I was in Phoenix."

Justin frowned. "How big a crowd?"

"Big enough," Alex said grimly. "And pillars of society all. Including Senator Rankin."

Justin let out a compressed breath.

"Well, that certainly muddies the water quite a bit more," he said.

"Indeed it does."

Their suspect list had just grown to immense proportions.

Chapter 18

"No warning this time," Alex said grimly as they started out in the morning in her grandfather's Mercedes; she hadn't even begun to do anything about replacing her own totaled car.

"No," Justin agreed, settling back in the passenger seat like a person who didn't usually travel in such style and wanted to enjoy every minute.

"No appointment," Alex went on. "Not in his office, not on his turf. I want to catch him by surprise and off guard."

"Fine," Justin said. "But he is a U.S. senator, with a lot of practice in obfuscation, so keep that in mind."

"So was Marion, and she didn't need or use obfuscation," she retorted. "*That's* what I'll keep in mind."

It had only taken her a few calls to find out the senator was playing golf with some friends today. And less time to decide that was perfect, she could get to him and he'd have nowhere to hide.

By eight they were at the country club. Justin grimaced as they drove past the entry to the clubhouse and saw the damaged pillar. Alex didn't even glance at it; she was utterly focused on the pursuit.

"Does everybody at this place drive a black Mercedes?" he asked.

Alex glanced at the cars they were passing in the lot, and indeed there were several in a row that looked like carbon copies of her grandfather's. A few more and it would look like a car dealer's lot. As it was, it was clearly a haven, not for the upwardly mobile but for the already arrived.

She laughed. He'd managed to distract her, for the moment at least. "Now you know why he prefers to drive his Range Rover. He got tired of having to read the plate every time to be sure he had the right one, or risk setting off a car alarm."

Once they reached the golf course, she pulled out her best club manners and her grandfather's name to get the woman at the pro club desk to tell them the senator's foursome had teed off early this morning, and had not yet checked back in.

"They should be coming to the eighteenth very soon," she said with a brilliant smile.

"I'll catch him there," Alex said, with an equal smile meant to charm. "I can tease him mercilessly about never breaking par."

She'd heard enough about the senator's golf game to guess that the comment would make the woman laugh.

It did. More important, she waved them through without any further questions. She wondered if the woman just trusted her because of her name, or wasn't up to speed on current security needs. She made a mental note to be sure G.C. took extra precautions whenever he came here.

Alex led Justin through the club and out the back French doors that looked out onto the course, turning to the left as soon as they were outside.

"Know where you're going, I gather?" Justin asked.

"Yes. My mother plays here. She dragged me out on occasion, when I was younger."

"Mmm."

Something about the way he made the sound made her look at him. And for a moment she saw the Dark Angel again, that wildly beautiful boy who'd grown up hard and tough and angry.

"Country clubs not a big part of your everyday life?"

"Mmm."

"Not mine, either."

He smiled.

"But," she added, "they are a part of my world. I don't participate, but they are there."

His steps slowed. She turned to face him.

"Worried I won't fit?" he asked.

She reached out and touched his cheek. "Worried that you're worried," she said softly.

A slow smile curved his mouth. "Don't. I'm long past worrying about finding a place in the world. I make my own."

She wanted to kiss him then and there, but knew they needed to focus. And if she kissed him…

"Save that thought," he said, looking at her face.

"Count on it," she whispered.

They went on, reluctantly. There was no sign of their quarry at the eighteenth hole, so they followed the carefully manicured path to the seventeenth.

"Is that the group?" Justin asked, pointing ahead.

She turned her head to look. After a moment she spotted the senator near the tee. "Yes."

"I thought they looked right. How do you want to play it?"

She'd been thinking about that. "Let me start out low-key," she said. "He might be surprised to see me, but I can put up a front that I'm here personally, as a member. Enough to maybe keep him off guard long enough to let something slip."

He nodded. "I'll hang back, then. Give me a sign if you feel like it's not going to work, and I'll come rattle the cage."

Rankin was indeed surprised to see her, and glanced rather nervously at the rest of his foursome, three men Alex didn't recognize, but she didn't give him time to think about it.

"I thought that was you, Senator," she said breezily. "How good to see you again!"

"Why, yes, of course," he stammered out. But he recovered quickly and poured on the charm. "It's good to see you again, too. How are you, Ms. Forsythe?"

"Oh, fine." The other men had moved away, clearly to give the senator some room. "I'm glad to be home."

"Ah, yes, how was your trip? Arizona, I believe your mother said?"

So he was going to play dumb, she thought. "Yes. Oh, by the way, thank you for telling Clarice Pennington where I was. I might have missed her otherwise."

Rankin frowned. "I don't recall telling her. Or her asking."

"Odd. She said it was you. Perhaps she heard it from someone else who heard it from you."

"No," he said, looking both thoughtful and worried in equal amounts. "I didn't say anything about your trip to anyone else."

Anyone else?

She was tired of waiting, tired of all this gentle probing. Tired of so many things in this town, where men like Rankin held the power because of who their friends were.

"You only told the one person it was important to,

then?" she asked, taking care to keep her tone light and casual.

It worked, to a point. He began to nod. Then he stopped himself short.

When he looked at her, there was actual fear in his eyes. Whoever he'd told, it was someone who had the capability to scare this man. And now he knew that she also knew there was someone with a great interest in her whereabouts and activities.

She knew immediately that he'd clammed up tight. He said nothing more and briskly suggested he should get on his way so he didn't hold up his foursome any longer. But she knew he was rattled and thought she'd better take a chance, since it was unlikely she'd catch him off guard again.

The instant Rankin looked away, she lifted one arm and held up a finger. Justin headed toward her quickly. Rankin heard him coming and frowned anew.

"Good morning, Senator," Justin said cheerfully. "I'm Special Agent Justin Cohen."

He flipped open his ID and badge holder and let the man see it. Rankin's eyes widened, and he glanced over his shoulder as if to see if his companions were close enough to see or hear. Alex held her breath; she hadn't expected him to come on like this, they didn't have any official backing on this, after all.

"Sorry to interrupt your conversation, especially with such a beautiful lady," Justin said, "but I'm afraid I need to ask you a couple of questions."

"She's an old family friend," Rankin said.

What an odd answer, Alex thought. Then she caught Justin's wink and realized the man was denying an intimate relationship with her. Alex bit back an astonished chuckle. You truly do learn to act like the company you keep, she thought.

"Questions about what?" Rankin asked belatedly.

"The murder of Marion Gracelyn."

That look of fear darted across his face again. "The FBI is opening that case again?"

Alex waited to see how Justin was going to get around that one.

"The possibility exists, depending on what I find out," he said smoothly.

Nicely dodged, Alex thought, and again stifled a grin.

"But why ask me? It happened years ago, and in Arizona." Then, as if he'd only just made the connection, he turned back to Alex. "I already told you everything I knew, which was nothing. Are you behind this? You and that book you're doing?"

"Ms. Forsythe," Justin said, "and her...book, aside, I want to know what you told one particular person in D.C."

"Nothing! I don't know what you're talking about."

"You want to go down with him, Senator?"

Oddly, that statement seemed to calm the man down. He was cool and appeared relaxed as he replied, "Really, Agent Cohen, you're misguided. I know nothing about Former Senator Gracelyn's death. Now if you'll excuse me, I've left my friends waiting too long already."

"My," Alex said as she watched him rejoin the rest of his group, "that was quite an abrupt change."

"Yes," Justin said sourly. "So much for that great idea. Sorry."

"No," Alex said, "we got something. Three some-things, in fact."

"What?"

"First, he inadvertently admitted he'd told at least one person about my trip to Arizona."

"But not who?"

"No. He caught himself before he let that slip."

"What else, then?"

"Why do you suppose he went so calm and cool at the end there?"

Justin shrugged. "I don't know. You have a theory?"

"I do," she said. "I think it was what you said."

"At the risk of sounding stupid...huh?"

"I think," she said slowly, still working it out in her mind, "when you said that about going down with him, whoever he is, it put Rankin back in control."

"Okay, now you've got me totally lost."

"I think it put him back in control because he's convinced that whoever it is will never go down."

Justin blinked. Then, softly, he said, "And the third thing?"

"He grabbed his cell phone and made a call the minute we walked away."

"So who would he be calling?" Justin asked as they walked along the outskirts of the country club grounds, along the Potomac River. "Who's he afraid of, and thinks everybody else should be afraid of, too? Except maybe your grandfather, of course."

Alex's mouth quirked. "I'm glad you realize that."

"I knew that the first time I met him."

Points for that, she thought.

"That's a short list," she said in answer to his question. "Especially in a town that builds careers out of tearing other people down."

"If you can't beat 'em, destroy 'em?"

"Pretty much," she said, her nose wrinkling in distaste.

He stopped, looking out at the bridge over the river, the bridge that led into the city.

"When I was growing up, I was always struggling to just survive long enough for Kelly to get us back together. This kind of life…it was something we never even knew existed, let alone dreamed about."

Alex knew he still grieved for his sister, who had tried so hard to take care of him after their parents died. Had tried so hard it killed her. Her death had been tangled up in the decades-old mess that had finally been revealed by Alex and her friends last year, and Justin finally had the truth he'd fought so long and hard for. But it didn't change the simple fact that his sister was dead and he missed her.

Not knowing what to say about such endless pain, she instead reached out and took his hand. "If she'd made it," she said, her voice quiet, "you wouldn't have cared about this kind of life. It's just...window-dressing. Family, and their love, that's the real thing."

He squeezed her fingers in response, a silent appreciation for her words that she'd learned to interpret. But he kept looking over toward Washington.

"Back then I never thought about this place much, what happened here or how it affected people throughout the country."

"You didn't miss much," she said. "A lot of the time it's not a very pretty process."

"Yeah." His voice was a little tight. "Now I have to play political games with the rest of them." He let out a compressed breath. "Can we get out of here?"

"You bet," she said quickly.

They were back in the car and headed for the main gate before Justin spoke again. "It's not that I'm jealous," he began.

"I never thought you were. It's just not your world."

"But it is yours."

"A small part of it. A part I'm happy to avoid whenever possible. I don't— Uh-oh," she said, cutting off her own words. "What's up here?"

Justin leaned forward to look ahead, where a blue, medium-size bus, canted at an odd angle, appeared to be blocking the driveway into the club parking lot. "Looks like a breakdown. Or a flat on that bus, whatever it is."

"That's the club shuttle bus," she said. "It picks up people who don't take their cars into the city, but want to squeeze in nine holes at lunch."

"Nice lunch break," Justin muttered.

"It also brings inner-city kids out to use the tennis courts and the pool," she said mildly.

"Oh," Justin said, sounding a little abashed.

She had to halt the car at the driveway, which was almost completely blocked. The driver of the shuttle was in front of it, scratching his head in puzzlement.

Some of the passengers had gotten off, others, mostly kids, were still aboard but clearly getting restless. She saw a tiny face at one window, a wide-eyed little girl who looked on the verge of tears.

Alex sighed and opened her door. The closer she got, the clearer it became that Justin's guess of a flat had been accurate. Three, in fact; the left front and the next set of double wheels behind that. Justin walked toward the flattened tires while she headed for the pacing driver, who seemed at a total loss.

"What happened?" she asked him as she got close. It was a young man, barely out of his teens, she guessed, and he seemed more than a little flustered.

"Had to be something in the road," the man said,

sounding a tiny bit defensive, "for all three of those tires to go flat at once."

"Did you hear it?"

"Heard a thump kind of sound, that's all."

Alex looked up the road, back where it had come from. About a block back, she saw something lying in the outside lane. She couldn't see what it was, but it was long and narrow, and protruded out a good three feet into the traffic lane. If the bus had come down that lane, it had to have gone over that thing. She'd go look at it, once everything calmed down a little here.

Justin walked over to her. "Tires are shredded," he reported succinctly. "Definitely not just a blowout. I'm going to check the undercarriage."

She nodded, and turned back to the young driver. "Have you called for help?"

"Uh, no, not yet. Guess I should, huh?"

Ya think? Alex muttered inwardly, but she only nodded; he was probably just rattled. And it could have been worse; he could have overcorrected and ended up rolling the bus, and then they really would have had a mess on their hands.

"Then we should probably get these folks off-loaded," she suggested.

He nodded quickly, and Alex suspected it was the "we" that had done it. He'd just felt alone, that's all, she thought.

She glanced back up the lane and frowned. She'd

changed angles and could now see that the elongated object in the roadway had teeth. Literal teeth.

A spike strip? Here?

Adrenaline shot through her. There could be no other meaning. This was no accident. There was deadly intent behind the placement of that piece of metal designed for one thing and one thing only: stopping any oncoming vehicle.

A new urgency filled her, and she had to work to keep her voice even and cheerful as she turned back to the bus and its occupants.

"Okay, everybody," she called out to the people on the bus, focusing on the restless kids. "Let's get you all inside so you can start having some fun instead of sitting out here on this bus."

A cheer went up. Happy chatter began as they filed off the damaged vehicle.

Alex gestured them over to the sidewalk.

She glanced once more at the spike strip. She'd have to tell Justin. Since his first instinct had been to check the undercarriage of the bus, he knew something wasn't right about all this. But why would somebody go after a bus like this?

Unless...the bus wasn't the target.

Alex's every nerve went on alert. The only targets she knew of here and now were her and Justin themselves. But nobody had known they were coming here. Had they been followed? She hadn't thought so, and Justin hadn't noticed a tail either, but—

An image, vivid and sharp, cut off her own thoughts. Rankin, reaching for his cell phone the moment they'd left him. She'd thought he'd been calling whoever was behind this, to warn him they'd been there. Maybe he had, and that person had called someone else.

And maybe the hunter hadn't followed them because he didn't need to. Maybe he'd simply waited for a call telling him where they were.

Her pulse was hammering now, and Alex gestured at the still chattering group to move faster, up onto the relative safety of the sidewalk.

A split second later the chatter was lost in the horrific sound as the bus exploded.

Chapter 19

Alex whipped around.

The bus was in flames.

Justin.

He was underneath.

Alex's heart slammed into her throat and she couldn't breathe. Her knees wobbled, and she felt a chilling wave of shock sweep over her.

You can't afford that! she ordered herself. Move. Now. Fast.

Years of training, both at the FBI and Athena kicked in, and she began to move. Fast. Fortunately, the passengers had already gotten off the bus, but they'd all still been gathered close by. Too close.

There were injuries at the very least, she was sure, probably some bad ones.

The driver was still off to one side, appearing to be unhurt, but looking dazed. That wasn't surprising, she thought; it appeared the cab portion of the vehicle had sustained the most damage.

"Call 911," she snapped at him. "Somebody who's not hurt check for injuries," she added, aiming at anybody still on their feet.

Her instinct was to find Justin, but she knew her job was to help the innocent victims. She and Justin were trained for this sort of thing, these people— especially the children—were not.

By now people were coming out of the buildings of the club, and the office building across the street. She saw some that were carrying cell phones, so she didn't worry about the dazed driver making any sense, if he'd even managed to call. Someone would get the message through to emergency services. The dispatchers were good, they would put the pieces together if they had to.

One of the adults who had been aboard the bus, a woman in what had once been a spotless designer suit, was already moving among the others, apparently following the order to check for injuries. She was doing it efficiently enough that Alex crossed that off her list for the moment.

The bus was burning fast now. Alex could hear at least one person screaming from inside. She ripped at the tail of her own shirt and tied a makeshift bandanna over her mouth and nose, grabbed up a bottle of water that had ended up on the ground, opened it swiftly and poured it all over herself as best she could.

Then she barreled up the rear steps of the bus, away from the wrecked cab, through the smoke and licking flames and toward the screaming.

She found the man in the back, lying on the bent floor of the bus with one leg pinned under a seat at an angle that told her it was probably broken. He was apparently the only one who hadn't been able to get off.

He clawed at her, still screaming. She tried to reassure him, but the smoke and heat was getting worse, and she had little time. She tried the rear emergency exit, but it was partially crumpled and didn't want to move. She backed up and kicked it as hard as she could. On the third try it budged slightly.

She braced herself on the backs of the two last seats for leverage. Swung both legs up and punched with both feet at once. The exit hatch seemed to shriek, then it gave. She was fuzzy-headed enough from the smoke now that it took her a moment to realize it was also being pulled from outside. People were helping now, bless them.

She turned back to the man on the floor, who had quieted now. Or passed out, she wasn't sure. She pushed at the crumpled seat, but it didn't move. She shifted position and put her shoulder into it, bracing her feet against the next seat, which was bent but seemed solid enough. She went nearly dizzy with the effort and the lack of air, but at last it gave, and she was able to pry the man free.

She bent and grabbed him under the arms. She knew it would have hurt horribly if he'd been conscious, so she was grateful that he wasn't.

It took a huge effort, and required more air than she could get amid the smoke, but she got him to the exit. Hands reached up to help, and once she felt them take him she let the man slip from her grasp.

Coughing and dizzy, her eyes streaming tears and knowing she had little time left herself, Alex made her way back to the front of the bus, checking each seat by feel since she could no longer see. In a seat toward the front, to her shock, she found a small, unmoving body.

A child.

A vivid image flashed through her mind, of a small, frightened face peering at her through one of the vehicle's windows. The little girl had been about here, toward the front of the bus.

Her heart in her throat now, Alex bent over the seat. She touched the small shape again. Alive? She couldn't tell. Couldn't see anything now through the smoke. She gathered the limp child up in her arms and headed for the door as fast as she could manage.

She slipped going down the steps, but someone steadied her, helped her balance, then lifted the frighteningly still burden from her arms. And then, at last, she could breathe again. But the moment she was clear she turned back to the bus. Dropped to the ground to peer underneath. Could see nothing amid the smoke that was now billowing down as well as up.

She blinked. Tried to focus, but her eyes were blurry from smoke.

"J—" Her throat was so raw she could barely speak. She swallowed and tried again. "Justin!"

She heard a sound. A groan?

She blinked, rubbed at her eyes, blinked again, and at last was able to see something. A shape, dark, still. It took everything left in her to hang on to some semblance of discipline and keep acting dispassionately.

She flattened herself on the ground and began to scramble under the smoking bus, propelling herself forward with knees and elbows. She was vaguely aware of jabs and stings as she made her way over debris. Didn't care.

And then she was there, touching him.

He groaned.

Adrenaline spurted through her. She moved swiftly then, running her hands over him, searching for injuries. She found no blood, no obvious broken bones. Ordinarily she would have waited for medical help, but the smoke was getting worse and she had to get him out of there before the fire hit the huge fuel tank.

She wasn't sure how she did it. She only knew it was Justin and it had to be done, so she did it. There was no room to maneuver, but she did it. There was no way to get leverage, but she did it. And the moment when, out in the sunlight again, he opened those turquoise eyes and looked up at her was like a full, deep breath of cool, clean air.

"Ouch," he said.

Alex couldn't help herself; she laughed. She knew she sounded giddy. She probably was, she admitted to herself. Giddy with relief that he was alive. Smokey, a bit grimy, maybe hurt, but alive.

He moved as if to get up. She gently pushed him back. "Take it easy." As she said it she realized she was hearing the sirens. "Medics are on the way."

"I'm okay. Just a little woozy and a bit singed."

"We'll let them decide if you're okay," she said.

"In command mode, are we?" he said, but he smiled when he said it and stayed put.

She put out a hand to touch a bloody spot on his head, but drew her hand back when she realized how grimy it was.

"Anyone killed?" he asked.

"I don't know."

"Hurt?"

"Some," she said. "I don't know how many or how bad. But it could have been worse, if the bomb had been in a different place, closer to the fuel tank."

"It wasn't a bomb."

Alex blinked. "What?"

She heard the shouting and scrambling as the fire

department arrived and went into action, but she didn't look. She focused on what Justin was saying.

"It wasn't a bomb. If it had been, I'd likely be dead. It was something fired."

Alex's eyes widened. "Fired? You mean like a rocket or something?"

"Yeah. An RPG, maybe. I heard the whistle right before it hit. I can't be sure where it came from. Sound was kind of muffled from under there."

Alex instinctively looked around, searching for any sign that a sniper might still be around. When she saw no suspicious movement, she began to look for anywhere a sniper with that kind of equipment might have hidden. The area around the scene was fairly open and lacking in cover except for the buildings of the club and the four-story office across the street.

And then the paramedics were there, hustling her out of the way as the firefighters tackled the bus and they began a triage of the injured. She went, knowing Justin was in better hands than hers for medical assessment.

She went to the other side of the still-smoking bus, knowing that the barrage of water and foam would quickly obliterate any evidence. Immediately she saw that Justin had been right. The gaping wound in the side of the bus was marked with an inward, not outward curve of bent, twisted and blackened metal.

Had they been wrong about this? she wondered. Were they dealing with the disgruntled general, or some other military type? Had someone there truly been so violently opposed to Athena back in the beginning that they would take out one of their most loyal supporters?

No time now, she reminded herself, and continued to study the damage.

The hole not only went inward instead of out, it was also, she noted, near the front. Thankfully the farthest it could have been from the fuel tank and still hit the vehicle. She also saw that her quick assessment had been accurate; if the driver hadn't gotten out to look at the tire damage, there was no doubt he would be dead, incinerated in the blast that had apparently been somewhat confined by the cockpit design of the driver's compartment.

It occurred to her then that this bore the same hallmark as the previous attacks: all the tools but lousy execution.

She hadn't really had time to think until now, hadn't had time to think about the possibilities—and probabilities—of this particular incident.

At first it had seemed like a simple vehicle breakdown. It had quickly become clear it was tampering, even sabotage, with the tire damage. She had no doubt now, when she looked at the object lying in the roadway in the bus's path, that it had been put there exactly for the purpose of stopping the vehicle.

The explosion had instantly taken it to another level altogether, she realized. And a second later she told herself not to assume that everything that happened everywhere around her was related to what she was working on.

And then she'd been too busy, too consumed with the rescue effort and worry about Justin to think about anything besides what she had to do.

She supposed there were other possibilities: foreign terrorism for one, in the forefront of everyone's mind and being discussed among the shocked survivors.

Or some kind of domestic terrorism, in resentful protest against the country club for the kind of success it stood for.

But she knew it wasn't. She knew it wasn't any of those other possibilities. Deep in her gut she knew that grenade had had one purpose: to stop this investigation. She guessed it was just bad luck for the hunter that while the first vehicle to run over their carefully planted spike strip had indeed converted them from moving to stationary targets, the vehicle had been a bus big enough to absorb more of the impact of the blast than a car would have.

If she and Justin had left a minute earlier or later, the shocked bystanders might be waiting for the coroner's wagon to pick up two dead federal agents and more.

"Are you all right?"

She turned to look at the young woman in the paramedic uniform who had come up beside her.

"I believe so," she said. Now that she thought about it, she felt a few twinges, but only minor ones, and a couple sore spots she guessed would become bruises. "My eyes and throat are the worst."

"Come along, then, and we'll rinse you out. And there are some people who'd like to thank you."

"What?"

"You are our heroine, aren't you? They kept talking about the redhead who went into the fire."

"Oh. Well. Somebody had to."

"Not everyone would."

The woman—her name badge read Tanya Arnold gestured at her to sit on the back bumper of the medic van.

"Look," she said, feeling the need to explain as the woman got out some bottles and sterile bandages, "I'm trained. FBI. It's what I do."

"I know. The other agent told us. But still, it was a very courageous thing to do. And because of you, a man who could have died is going home to his family, and a young mother still has hers."

"The child?" Alex asked. "I'm sorry, I didn't think to ask."

"You've been busy," the young woman said with a grin. "And yes, the little girl's going to be all right. Thanks to you. Now hold still."

The saline the medic used to rinse out her eyes felt cool and clean and welcome. Gentle hands patted at her cheeks, blotting at the overflow.

"What about Justin? The agent?"

"He's going to be all right, too, although we're

going to transport him for a CT scan, just to be sure. He was close to the explosion in a confined space, and we don't want to miss a possible concussion."

She nodded, glad they were being careful. "How are the rest of the passengers?"

"Some fairly serious injuries, some minor. But nobody was killed outright, and in a situation like this, that's good news."

Alex nodded. Her vision had now cleared. She could see the crowds that had gathered around the perimeter, behind the yellow tape that was ubiquitous at such crime scenes. Some of those gathered were obviously passersby of the type unable to actually pass by such an event. But many of the others were people who, judging by their uniforms and golf attire, had been drawn out of the club by the explosion or the ensuing commotion.

Including, she noticed as she scanned the crowd, the senator's foursome.

Threesome, she corrected herself with interest.

The three men Rankin had been playing with were there among the others, peering at the still-smoldering bus with obvious grim fascination. The only one missing was Rankin. Alex could only think of one reason for that.

He'd already known what was going to happen.

Chapter 20

Justin indeed had a concussion, albeit a mild one. He wasn't happy when the nurse came in to tell him they were admitting him to the hospital for at least twenty-four hours.

When he protested rather crankily, she merely smiled and promised mildly to make it forty-eight if he didn't cooperate.

Justin frowned.

Alex told him to grow up and quit giving people who were trying to help him a hard time.

Unexpectedly he grinned at her. "I like it when you get all proprietary."

The nurse chuckled, and Alex blushed. "Ah...love,"

said the nurse, teasing them both. That made Alex feel better. Obviously he was going to be okay, if they were joking with him.

"That's enough fun," the nurse said, "now you need to rest."

"But—"

"Hush," Alex said. "She's right, so I'll be leaving now."

"Come back?" he said, his voice so over-the-top hopeful that she had to laugh.

"Later," she promised. Then, in a very loud whisper, she added, "I'll sneak you in a burger and fries."

His grin widened. He looked at the nurse. "I love that woman," he told her.

"I can see that," the smiling woman in blue scrubs said.

Alex escaped before further embarrassment befell her. Why she was embarrassed she wasn't quite sure. Perhaps it was because she wasn't used to such public declarations of love.

Especially when they haven't really been made in private yet, she thought as she headed to the Alexandria house, a place she hadn't seen much of lately.

She felt exhaustion hovering, but knew it was mental and emotional rather than physical, so fought it off. She pulled into the drive of the house, thinking it odd how unfamiliar it suddenly seemed to her.

She gathered up her not inconsiderable load of gear and headed inside and to the family room that had a big table and, more important, the most comfortable chair in the place.

Once there, she kicked off her shoes and unloaded her laptop and satchel and the other odds and ends she'd acquired. Then she headed for the shower and a concerted effort to rid herself of the smell of the explosion and toxic smoke. She'd managed—barely—to dodge the detectives from the local police, giving them a statement with the essentials only and her card, saying she needed to go check on her fellow agent. They'd let her go then, but she knew she'd be hearing from them again soon.

Out of the shower and feeling better, she returned to the family room and began to unload her satchel, more determined than ever that the answer was in this pile of papers and that she was damned well going to find it. This was the real reason she'd left the hospital. That was hardly the place to spread all this out for anyone to see. Otherwise she never would have left Justin.

She poured some soda water, ice-cold and soothing to her still raw throat. She set up her laptop on a side table, signed on and checked mail, found nothing that couldn't wait. Saw that the police had called while she'd been in the shower and decided she'd postpone that callback for a while.

She pulled her bathrobe tighter around her and settled into the comfortable chair with a stack of notes and papers to begin anew. Again. Maybe going through it again in these surroundings would help. There were few distractions here, no horses that needed riding, no stalls that needed cleaning. Only flowery wallpaper to avoid looking at, and expensive knickknacks to use as paperweights.

Not even any snacks to nibble on—she might truly have to do that burger and fries later—nothing to do but concentrate.

When her cell phone rang an hour or so later, it was a welcome interruption. She was tired of feeling stupid. It was Pepper, keeping her promise to stay in touch.

"You're sure you're all right? That was so awful."

For a moment Alex thought she somehow knew about the bus explosion already, but then realized she was probably talking about the incident after the party.

"I'm fine, really. Thanks."

"Good, because I'm calling to invite you to a little thing we're having at the house next week. And bring your mysterious Justin with you. I want to meet him."

Oh, boy, meet the friends and family.... She started to dodge by saying he was in the hospital, but realized quickly that that would give rise to more questions than she wanted to answer right now.

"I'll talk to him about it," she said instead.

"Do," Pepper encouraged her. "There will be lots of your old friends here. Marla, Jen, oh, and I invited Charlene Laroque, sans Pierre, of course. Although I don't know if she'll come. She's so embarrassed."

"Understandable," Alex said. "I'll let you know, Pepper, but in any case, thanks so much for asking."

As she disconnected she found she meant it. Maybe not everything from this part of her life was so bad. Pepper was a nice person, despite the propensity to gossip.

She settled back in her chair and began yet again: the lists of names, the criminal case records and enemies made, the senatorial record and more enemies made. But Marion had made friends, as well, the victims of those criminals and their families, and the constituents she had always worked so hard for.

She spread the lists out, remembering what Justin had joked about, shaking all this stuff until the answer fell out. Right now it didn't seem like a half-bad idea. She pulled out the notes from the original murder case file, and had the thought that she should call Eric Hunt to see if anything new had occurred to him, now that the case had been perking in his mind again after all those years.

She'd do it as soon as she had this sorted out, she thought. Quickly she went through the rest of the pile until she reached the bottom, and the most recent item, the list Kayla had faxed her, of the stolen or missing library cards. It didn't really fit in any of the piles she already had, so she set it to one side.

Then she looked at it again, something nibbling at the edge of her memory.

Pepper's voice echoed in her ears.

I invited Charlene Laroque.

And her own, asking about Charlene and her husband.

They have a daughter, don't they?

She looked at the list again, not scanning this time but reading each name. The list was in chronological, not alphabetical, order so there was no way to speed up the process.

And finally, near the bottom of the third column, she found it.

Alex's gut tightened. She went back to her laptop and quickly looked up the number for the library in Athens. Called, and asked for Mr. Lang.

"Alexandra Forsythe, as I live and breathe."

Alex nearly laughed aloud as memories from Athena days flooded her. Every girl in her class had had a crush on the hunky Mr. Lang, back when he'd first started at the small library. From what Kayla had said, he was no less hunky now than he had been then. There had been a marriage in between that, according to rumor, had ended tragically, although no one seemed quite clear on exactly how. But he hadn't seemed inclined to reenter the dating pool, despite the efforts of many to lure him in.

"It's good to hear your knack for drama hasn't changed," she said.

"I'm wounded, girl. And don't think I've forgiven you for not becoming the star of stage and screen I know you could have been."

Alex did laugh then; in addition to playing a mean game of touch football for a local league, he had always attended the youth productions at the Athens Theater Group, and was unfailingly encouraging. When she'd appeared on stage in fellow Cassandra Darcy Steele's amazing makeup as the witch in *Macbeth*, he'd told her she was brilliant, nearly as brilliant as her makeup artist.

"Now," he said, "I presume you're calling about that little situation our illustrious lieutenant contacted me about?"

"Yes. The reservation on that computer."

"I know what you're going to ask, Alex. And you know I can't tell you who the card that reserved that machine belongs to. Not without a subpoena or a warrant."

"And I'd rather not put you in that position," she said. "So let me suggest this. I won't ask you to give me a name, or even a number. But if I give you the number I suspect, can you at least tell me if I'm right or wrong?"

He was silent for a long moment.

"It's a murder investigation," she said. "It may have happened a long time ago, but it still matters. And whoever did it is still out there, because he's tried to stop me. Is still trying."

"Alex—"

"He blew up a bus today, David," she said, using his first name for the first time ever. "With kids onboard. It was only sheer luck, timing and bad aim that kept any or all of them from being killed."

She heard him take in a long, deep breath. Then she decided to fire the last round, if for no other reason than to put it out loud into words for herself to hear, to test, to try on.

"He put…the man I love in the hospital. I want to stop him. I have to. I'm *going* to stop him. You can just make it happen a little sooner. Maybe before somebody else gets hurt."

More silence, then a rueful sigh. "You Athenas are all cut from the same cloth, aren't you?"

"Yes, we are."

"All right. Hang on."

He didn't sound happy, but he was going to do it. She heard a click as he put her on hold, and then the recorded promo for an upcoming reading fair. It was interrupted after about thirty seconds when he came back.

"Give me the number."

She read the card number off the list in her hand. When she finished there was silence. Then a sigh. She felt for him, she really did. He was in a difficult place. But neither he—nor she—could change that, not anymore. The world was what it had become, and sometimes difficult choices had to be made.

"It's a match," he finally said.

Alex let out the breath she'd been holding. "Thank you, David. It was the right thing to do."

"Sure." He sounded beyond grim.

"It was," she reiterated. "This time. If there's a next time, I expect you to fight just as hard."

It took a moment, but when he spoke, his voice was lighter. "Oh, I will."

"I know."

As she hung up, Alex took a moment to wish an Athena on David Lang, too. She thought he could handle it.

And then she sat there with the list in her hand, the list that confirmed to her what she'd suspected, what they'd been struggling so long and hard to find out.

Who had been behind the murder attempts on first her, then her and Justin both.

Who had been willing to risk killing two federal agents.

Who had been willing to sacrifice a busload of innocent people, including children, in yet another attempt to keep them at bay.

Who had murdered Senator Marion Gracelyn.

She knew some would say that she was crazy to even try to bring this man down. You just didn't mess with people at his level, they would say.

Watch me, she thought, anger boiling up inside her. *You just watch me.*

Chapter 21

Alex waited for her temper to ebb before she picked up the phone and made the first of what she knew would be many phone calls. She knew this was going to be huge. While last year's investigation that had grown out of Rainy's murder had been big, much of it had been below the public radar. This was likely to be the highest profile thing she would ever encounter.

And that meant planning. Lots of it. This was going to have to be approached like a military strike, she thought. She had to think of every possibility and prepare for it. She had to cover all the ways her quarry could evade responsibility. She had to line up all the dominoes so they fell in the right direction, and with enough weight to take out that last, biggest domino.

And Alex knew the fall of that final domino was going to reverberate in places she didn't even know about.

She had the sudden need to talk to Justin, and only the knowledge that he did truly need to rest and would be in better shape tomorrow stopped her from calling.

There's time, she told herself. It's been ten years, it can wait another day or two.

It's more important that this go down perfectly, she thought. And that was going to take a perfect plan. Which was going to take time.

She sat down and opened a fresh page on her laptop. She began typing notes furiously, stopping only to copy and paste segments in a different order. Every note, every report, every theory, became crucially important now, because of the scrutiny it would all inevitably come under. And now that she had the last piece of the puzzle, the pattern became clear, and each piece fit with a solidness that made it impossible not to believe.

When she was done, she locked away the original documents and packed up her laptop. She gathered several items to put in her satchel. She called and caught G.C. on his way out.

"It's just a meeting of the Hunt Club board," he said. "You should come, you know they'd love to see you."

"I didn't think they've ever forgiven me for not making the run for the Olympic team."

He chuckled. "They seem to have forgotten that. Now they just say that you would have made it and leave it at that."

She laughed, but knew she sounded as tightly wound as she was feeling. And her grandfather knew her too well to miss it.

"Alex? What is it? Is it Justin?"

"No, no." But interesting that he assumed that first, she thought. "It's something else. Big."

"What?"

She took a deep breath and let it out. Once she told G.C., the ball would be rolling. There'd be no turning back. She'd better be damned sure she was right.

She was.

"I can't talk about it on the phone. I'm on my way to the farm."

There was the barest fraction of a second's pause before her beloved grandfather said, "I'll let them know I won't be there. I'll be waiting for you."

Bless you, G.C., she thought.

"I love you," she said.

"And I you. Drive carefully, and let me know if there will be any planned delays."

She didn't miss the implication, that if she was late and didn't call, he'd assume something had happened.

"I will."

She loaded up and headed for G.C.'s car, which she'd picked up at the country club after she'd left the hospital. With her grandfather's words echoing in her mind, she went over the car carefully, looking for any sign of tampering or anything that didn't belong. Finally satisfied, she got in.

Wanting to be able to pay full attention to possible threats on the road, she phoned the hospital before starting out. She got the good-natured nurse who was still on duty, and was told Justin was, finally, sleeping. She disconnected and pulled out of the driveway, concentrating on her driving from here on.

She made it without incident. G.C. was indeed waiting. He greeted her with a hug that was a bit stronger, a bit longer than usual. She hugged him back, knowing that they were both saying so much without saying a word.

Then he led the way into his office, where Alex set up her laptop. Knowing her grandfather preferred to read hard copy, she turned on his wireless printer and, when she had her multiple-paged theory called up, sent it. A second later the printing began, and a couple minutes later she handed him the document, keeping only the last page for herself.

As he sat down behind his desk, Alex curled up in her favorite chair, the green leather wingback beside the fireplace. She thought about reading through everything again at the same time he was, but right now it seemed too much. She already knew it all by heart, anyway. There was only one thing to do, and that was wait for the opinion of the man who had made her the woman she was.

She'd left her conclusions out of it, wanting him to reach the same conclusion she had without any prompting from her. If he reached a different one, then she'd know she'd either misinterpreted something, or he knew something she didn't, or she'd simply screwed up.

But if he did reach the same conclusion…

Desperate for something else to think about while he was reading, Alex turned her mind to the only thing powerful enough to take her mind off this mess.

Justin.

Like someone testing the waters of an unknown sea, she took out the memory of how she'd felt when she'd feared he was dead under the burning hulk of that bus. She remembered it vividly, because the only other time in her life when she'd felt such fear, such wrenching, gut-shaking fear, was when G.C. had been in the hospital for what they'd feared was a heart attack. It hadn't been, but Alex would never forget the feeling, so intense it had spilled over from the mental to the physical, making her knees weak.

I guess that tells you something, she told herself. It was time to quit running. Time to face how she felt about him, time to give in and admit that she had fallen, and fallen hard.

She smiled inwardly as an image of her sister Cassandras came to her, of their expressions if she told them this. She could see so clearly the rolling eyes, the pitying head shakes. "Good grief, girl," they would say, "do you think we don't know that?"

Looking back, it was fairly clear, she supposed. It had only been her own muddled outlook on relationships, inspired by her mother's efficiency at mucking them up, that had made her so resistant.

Thank goodness Justin was so patient.

Of course, the Dark Angel had learned patience the hard way. He—

"My God."

G.C.'s quiet, shocked exclamation snapped her out of her reverie. She sat up straight and turned to meet her grandfather's gaze. She'd rarely in her life seen him even taken aback, but now he looked stunned. And the name he muttered told her he'd reached that same conclusion. She didn't know whether to be glad or saddened.

"Yeah." She knew she sounded glum, but it was mostly weariness at the very idea of the task ahead.

"I won't insult you by asking if you're sure."

"I wish I wasn't."

She handed him that last page, the grid she'd set up with all the incidents from Marion's murder forward down one side, and all the possible suspects across the top. Each square where a definite connection could be shown or inferred between suspect and incident was blacked out with a big *X*.

Only one name had a complete column of black *X*s beneath it.

And then, with the energy that astounded others of his age, G.C. said briskly, "You're going to need help. If this is going to happen, if we're going to take him down, every last duck has to be in a row."

"I know." She rattled off the list of calls she had in mind. He nodded, and added a few of his own.

"When?" he asked.

"If circumstances don't dictate otherwise, as soon as Justin is able. He deserves to be in on this."

"Yes, he does." He gave her a sideways look. "And I'll say this now and then butt out. I wouldn't mind having that boy in the family."

Alex blushed but held her grandfather's gaze steadily. "I don't think I would, either," she said. "We're working on it."

"Good." G.C.'s tone was gruff but belied by his wide smile. He quickly became serious again as they turned back to the plan.

"I wish Josie were here," Alex said, naming another fellow Cassandra, who designed planes in the U.S. Air Force. "I feel like we need an engineer to put this together."

"We'll manage," G.C. said. Then with a shake of his head he added, "It has to be done."

"Yes. It does."

The briskness came back into his voice. "Let's get on with it, then."

She understood how he felt. He'd been a fixture in this town for thirty years, there wasn't an elected official in D.C. who didn't know and curry favor with Charles Forsythe. So it had to feel very strange to him, to be sitting here with his granddaughter, plotting against a part of that very establishment.

But she didn't know anybody better able to pull it off. There would be justice for Marion Gracelyn at last, and the man who had once been half in love with her would do it.

With her newfound understanding of love, she thought it most fitting.

Alex smiled at the woman at the desk in the outer room of the senator's office.

"I really appreciate him making time for me," she said sweetly.

"He was more than happy to, Ms. Forsythe. Ah," she added as a light on the desk phone went out. "There, he's clear from that call to the ambassador. You can go right in now."

Alex nodded. She supposed for someone who hadn't grown up hearing the names of ambassadors and prime ministers and presidents bandied about when discussing guest lists, this might be intimidating. But if that someone knew what this man had done, she suspected the intimidation would quickly give way to anger.

She wasn't angry. She'd gone past that. In fact, she was ice-cold, focused only on the job ahead, on what had to be done to achieve the goal. Everyone and everything was in place, and the only thing left was for her to start the snowball down the hill.

She stepped through the door with the brass plaque. She'd been in senators' offices before. This one was a bit more elegant, full of expensive antiques, and more self-aggrandizing, with a collection of trophies and memorabilia from around the world, and photographs of the room's occupant with virtually every famous face on the planet, but otherwise it was much the same.

The man behind the desk stood, an engaging smile on his face. He held out a hand, greeting her jovially. If he was surprised at her appearance, or if he had any concerns about her request to see him, it didn't show. He gestured her to a seat in front of his huge, weighty desk, and in a show of unconcern, took the other chair beside her, not even putting the barrier between them.

That overconfidence is going to be the end of you, she said to herself.

"How nice to see you again," he said.

"Hello, Senator."

"How's your grandfather? I keep meaning to call him."

"He's who he is," she said. "There's no artifice with him. No hidden agendas or skeletons in the closet."

The senator's brow creased slightly, but that was the only sign he saw anything untoward in her words.

"We should get together for lunch." He patted his ample girth with a chuckle. "Although, some would say I should stay away from the table."

"More golf," she suggested.

He laughed, relieved at what he clearly thought was a joke. "Good idea, Alexandra. Good idea. Now, what can I do for you? Need some help on that book of yours?"

Alex noted that the cover rumor was still alive and well. Decided to use it.

"I would like to run a story line past you for comment," she said.

"Fine, fine," he said expansively, and waved for her to go on.

"It's about this man who has for years abused the public trust. But he hides it so well, has his constituents so blinded that he keeps getting reelected, so often that he's come to think he's invincible, untouchable. He believes he's the unannointed king of a country that has no king. But he acts as if it does, and as if his simply wanting something should make it so. And finally, he becomes so convinced of his own royalty, that when a single voice begins to speak against him, when one brave soul stands up for what's right instead of the status quo, he stomps on that voice with no more care or concern than if it had been an ant."

He said nothing. His expression, practiced and cool from years of playing the game he'd practically invented didn't change. But something cold, hard and very, very frightening glinted in his eyes as he stared at her unblinkingly.

She wasn't about to stop now. "He gets away with

it, for years. He's sure he will never be caught. Perhaps, in time, he even manages to convince himself that he's done nothing wrong, that he'd merely removed an impediment to his vision. And his vision, of course, must be implemented, for the good of all, since he is the only one who can see what's best."

"That's quite a tale," the senator said. "You have a knack for fiction."

She ignored the comment. She was an Athena, and she wasn't about to be intimidated into silence, not even by this man.

"But then one day someone goes poking around the closet he's hidden that particular skeleton in. And no matter how he swats at them, they won't stop or go away. He becomes more frantic, until he loses all rationality and panics. He tries to kill agents of the very government he's supposed to represent. And then, even more unbalanced, he risks blowing up a dozen innocent people, including six children, in the effort to save himself."

"I believe I've spared you all the time I can for this quite fictional tale you're weaving."

Again she ignored him. "But do you know what happened? Instead of saving himself, he hung himself. He went that one step too far, gave those pests just that extra bit of time they needed to get that closet door open. And now they've got him."

"Enough," he said, in a booming voice that would ring familiar to hundreds of thousands across the country. "I agreed to see you, out of respect for your grandfather, but it's clear you're wasting my time."

"Actually," she said, "you're going to have plenty of time on your hands, Senator. More than you know what to do with. And don't worry about that belly of yours," she added. "Where you're going, they'll take care of that, too."

"How dare you!" He leaped to his feet. Alex was sure it had been a very long time since anyone had spoken to him in that tone. "I'll not take such insolence from you, no matter who your grandfather is!"

"Oh, you will," Alex whispered, rising slowly, leisurely, and for the first time letting every bit of her anger and disgust into her voice. "Because I'm not here as the granddaughter of Charles Forsythe. Nor am I here because of some nonexistent book. I'm here as the FBI agent who is going to take you down, and it's long past due."

"Get out."

"Was she gaining too much support? Were you afraid she was going to become the opposition's voice, that she would make the country see you for what you are?"

He called loudly for his aide. Alex didn't worry.

"Or was it simpler? Did she just get in your way? One too many of your pet bills voted down because of her? One too many of your pork-barrel riders exposed?"

He spun around and stabbed at the intercom console on his desk. He yelled into the speaker. He got the response Alex suspected. Nothing.

"Fine," he snarled. "I'll throw you out myself."

"Why don't you just kill me, like you did Marion?" Alex suggested. "Isn't that how you get rid of people who get in your way?"

"You're insane. You have no proof of any of this."

It was the claim Alex had been waiting for. "Proof? You want proof?"

She took a step toward him. She was nearly as tall as he was, and a lot more fit. She held up her hand in front of his reddened face, and began to tick off items.

"E-mail traced to a computer in your offices. Proof that that same computer hacked into mine for my travel and hotel data. Cell phone records, showing calls from numbers assigned to you to the man who tried to kill me out in the desert, and the man who tried to run me down with my own car here. Phone records, post office box records, here and in Phoenix, library computer records, all released under subpoena. All with times corresponding to the attacks you orchestrated."

"What is this, some kind of political conspiracy? Do you really think you can bring *me* down?"

"I don't have to, Senator. You've already done it yourself. We've got the man you hired ten years ago. And the man you hired to kill that man. We've got the money trail on their payments. We've got the details on that RPG you arranged to have fall off a military transport truck. We've got testimony of everyone you sucked into your evil little world. You thought you'd stay safe by parceling it all out, didn't you? Thought as long as nobody knew the whole, you'd be safe."

"You're insane."

Her voice dropped as anger vibrated through her. "Insanity," she nearly hissed, "is using, God damn you, your own granddaughter. Using her library card to communicate with your hired killer."

The senator's face reddened even further at her last words.

"Oh, yes, we know it all." It had taken them two weeks to pull it all together, but they did have it all now. And it would, as it already had in some quarters, stun the country. She continued to slam him with all of it, the list of all the things they'd uncovered seemingly endless.

"Shut up," he finally screamed.

"Give it up, Senator. It's over."

"You'll never make any of this stick."

"Still feeling Teflon coated?" she said. "It won't last. Because you see, we have the final nail for your coffin. A signed confession from someone quite familiar to you. In fact, he's right there in that picture, next to you."

He looked at the framed photograph of himself with the then-president and several others.

"That weasel," he whispered. "I should have known he couldn't be trusted."

"When you make these kind of choices, Senator, no one can be trusted."

She saw the change come over his face, then saw his expression morph into that of a cornered rat.

"You're right," he said, backing away carefully. "Sometimes the only one you can trust is yourself."

"You should have just killed her yourself. Then you really might have gotten away with it."

"I'll still get away with it," he said as his hand darted into a desk drawer and came up with a handgun, "as long as you don't leave this building."

"I take it back," she said.

"Oh, you think it's that easy?" he said as he waved the small, silver weapon at her. "Recant and I'll let you walk out of here?"

"I didn't mean that. I meant about not trusting you." He looked puzzled. "I did. I trusted you to do something exactly this stupid."

"We'll see about that. You and I are going to take a drive now."

"No, thanks. Some people I just won't get in a car with."

He swore then, a foul assessment of her and women in general.

"Your world's just not the same anymore, is it?" she said with mock sympathy. "It was better when all women were only good for one thing."

He swore again, and gestured at her with the gun. She smiled.

"You really should keep up with the times, Senator," she said cheerfully. She flicked at the small American flag lapel pin on her jacket. "Camera," she said. "And microphone. Amazing what they can do these days."

He stared at her, at the pin, disbelief on his face. "Did you really think I'd come in here unprepared? Is your opinion of all women really that low?" Then she spoke into the lapel pin. "Stop me before I get on a soap box."

The door behind them, into the outer office, swung open. The senator swung around to look, but Alex kept her eyes on his face. She knew the moment when her grandfather walked in by the sudden blanching of the man's face. And then he seemed to crumple before her eyes, as if all the pomposity and arrogance had truly been mere hot air, which was escaping, now that the world would know what he'd become.

"I can't believe that even you have sunk this low," G.C. said.

"Go back to your farm," the senator retorted, but although it was clearly meant to be an insult there was no spirit in it.

Next through the door was Justin. He winked at her, and she smiled back. Then she nodded at the beaten man. Justin took the cue, walked over and put a hand on the Armani-clad shoulder.

"Senator Eldon Waterton, you are under arrest."

Chapter 22

"Leave it to Alex to rock the world," Kayla said.

"Somebody needs to remind you you're supposed to be a lab rat." That was Darcy Steele.

"Couldn't you find a killer with a higher profile than the most powerful senator in the country?" Josie Lockworth chimed in.

The teasing was coming from all sides, and Alex didn't even try to deflect any of it. These were her beloved sister Cassandras, and she was too delighted to see them. Especially back here at Athena, the place they all thought of as their home, finally out from under the shadow of its founder's brutal murder.

She looked around, eyes stopping on each woman

so dear to her—dark-haired, honey-skinned Kayla; petite, bubbly Darcy who finally had the smile back on her face after escaping forever her abusive husband; and trim, brunette Josie, who had a few days' leave from the air force base in California. Missing were golden-haired Sam, who was off on another CIA adventure, no doubt, and of course Tory Patton, whose TV news show kept her tied to New York for the moment. They'd called Sam and Tory and left messages for them to enjoy whenever they could check in. And of course, they and Marion Gracelyn's family had all been filled in on this latest Athena triumph.

Athena Force had banded together once more, and it felt good.

Christine Evans called for their attention by flicking her champagne glass with a fingernail.

"Enough, all of you incorrigibles," she said with a laugh. "I need your attention. I want to propose a toast. To Alex, for bringing Athena out of the darkness, and bringing justice at last to the woman who had the dream and made it happen."

"Here, here," they chorused, and clinked glasses together.

The phone rang and Christine went to answer it as Darcy called out, "Speech, speech."

"Oh, please," Alex laughed.

"Yeah, come on, girlfriend," Kayla urged.

"Look," Alex said, "I didn't do this alone. Besides

my grandfather, Christine helped. Kayla was with me every step of the way, and Eric Hunt was beyond helpful. Samantha pulled some of our evidence out of a deep, dark computer hole. And Tory provided that rarest of creatures, an honest news report. And Josie's little sister, Diana, warning the White House so they were ready."

"And Justin?" Kayla said archly.

"Of course." Alex kept her voice level. "Not only did he go through all this and get hurt in the process, he's the one who got Senator Rankin to confess that he'd been the point man all along."

"And that's all he did?" Josie said, waggling an eyebrow.

"Oh, he did enough. More than enough." Alex finally lost her cool then, and the Cassandras hooted as she blushed furiously.

Her cell phone rang, and she was silently thankful for the interruption. And for once she wasn't wishing it was Justin; that would just let her in for even more harassment.

She looked at the Caller ID, and smiled as she flipped open the phone.

"Eric."

"Hi, Alex. I just got through your full report. That was an amazing bit of work you did."

"More like rattling a lot of cages until the snake fell out."

"Whatever, it worked. You did it."

"I had something you didn't," she said. "I grew up in that world, or on the fringe of it, anyway. I knew just how evil those big boys can get."

"Thanks, but I don't need the excuses. I know I was in way over my head back then. Now I'd like to think I'd do better."

"Don't think it, Eric. Know it. You're a fine cop. They're lucky to have you. And if it's what you want, go for that sergeant's exam Kayla told me is coming up in a couple of months. You've got the stuff."

For a moment there was silence. And then a quiet "Thank you," that fairly echoed with sincerity.

She'd barely hung up when someone called her name.

"Alex?"

It was Christine, holding the phone out to her. She took it, wondering who'd be calling her here.

"Alex? It's Allison. I wanted to thank you. More than words can say."

"No thanks necessary," Alex assured her.

"Thank you, anyway. From me, my brother and my father. He's at peace for the first time in years."

"I'm glad," Alex said, meaning it.

"If you ever get tired of that FBI lab, you call me. Promise."

Alex was puzzled, but said, "Okay. I will. Did anything turn up about that other situation?"

"No. Not yet."

After another round of thank-yous and a repetition

of her sharing of the credit, Alex hung up and went back to the party. She hadn't realized how much she missed the camaraderie until she was back here among her closest friends.

"Athena Force," she announced, "needs to get better at staying in touch."

They all agreed, and the chatter about how to do that began. Alex joined in, smiling and laughing with her sister Cassandras.

But beneath the feeling of closure and camaraderie was a single, hovering thought, suspended in the back of her mind as if by a thread. A silken thread like that of the spider whose scribbled image she couldn't quite erase from her mind.

Marion had been blackmailed, and they still don't know by whom. Or over what. But she had the feeling that spider was the key.

I guess the Cassandras aren't quite through with history yet.

* * * * *

Silhouette Bombshell and the women of
ATHENA FORCE
have more thrilling adventures to share!
Don't miss the next story in this popular
continuity series, featuring CIA agent
Samantha St. John
and her Russian-spy twin sister, Elle.
LOOK-ALIKE
By Meredith Fletcher
Available May 2006
wherever Silhouette Books are sold.

Athena Academy for the Advancement of Women
Outside Athens, Arizona

Controlling the outrage that stirred within her, Samantha St. John sat at the conference table across from Alexandra Forsythe and Allison Gracelyn.

"I know you're angry, Sam." Alex spoke softly, in her professional voice, and that irritated Sam more.

At five-feet-eight inches tall with long, curly red-gold hair and blue eyes, Alex was a hard woman to miss in a crowd. Currently, she lived in Washington, D.C., and worked for the FBI.

"You're right," Sam said in a quiet, controlled

voice. "I'm angry. I had a vacation planned with my sister. A quiet time where we could get away and get to know more about each other—"

"We didn't plan this," Alex said.

"—and, instead, I ended up in Amsterdam, in an area that is an absolute zoo and freak show where people sell their freedom and self-respect for cash," Sam continued. "And then Elle nearly gets blown up while retrieving the man you two want to question—"

"We didn't know that was going to happen," Allison objected.

"—and now, after she's risked her life to help me do a task I still don't even know the reason for," Sam said, "you've turned her away like you don't trust her. You bet I'm angry."

"There's a reason for our not including Elle at the moment," Alex assured her.

"Oh, really?" Sam stared at her friend. She couldn't remember ever being so pissed at Alex. Or any of the Cassandras, for that matter. "Maybe you'd like to share that reason with me."

"I can't at the moment."

Abruptly Sam stood to leave. "Then I can't stay." She turned and headed for the door. She was so mad she was shaking. She couldn't remember the last time she had been this near to being out of control. The realization scared her. Without control she was a victim, and victims had to go along with whatever happened to them. She'd learned that growing up in foster homes.

"Sam," Alex called. "Please don't leave."

Pausing at the door, Sam turned to face the other two women. "You've known me for a long time. Both of you. I've never asked for much. From either of you. Or from anyone. I gave you help on this without ever asking why or what it was about. Elle gave me the same thing. Simply because we're family. Something I thought you of all people would understand. You told me there was a possibility that what we were doing had something to do with my parents."

Alex fixed her with her open, honest gaze. There wasn't a hint of deceit in her blue eyes. "This *is* about your parents, Sam. That's why this is so hard. The answers you want are complicated. We're still dealing with them ourselves. Please be a little more patient."

"Why couldn't Elle be here?" Sam asked. "My mother and father were her parents, too. That's what this is about, right? My parents?"

"Yes," Alex said, "and no."

Sam blew out an angry breath.

"I told you it was complicated," Alex said.

"You're aware that your mission was initiated by Alex's recent investigation into my mother's death," Allison said calmly.

For the first time, Sam saw that Allison looked frayed around the edges.

"We sifted through a lot of old evidence while looking for Marion's murderer," Alex said. "We also turned up several e-mail communications from

someone who only signed the messages 'A.' Most of
those communications were fragmented and hidden
in code we believe Marion created herself. We have
been able to decipher some of them, but not all."

"I'm still working on it," Allison said. "But it seems
my mother was even more clever than I had known."

Curiosity nibbled at Sam's anger. Mysteries had
always appealed to her.

"My mother was being blackmailed," Allison said.
"Part of those blackmail threats included you."

INVISIBLE RECRUIT
by Mary Buckham

She'd transitioned from high-society
woman to undercover operative,
but Vaughn Monroe's first
assignment throws her right
back into the jet-set world she
stepped away from. Will she be able
to capture the elusive criminal who
knows a little too much about her...?

**IR-5: Five women,
trained to blend in,
become a powerful
new weapon.**

*Available May 2006
wherever Silhouette
books are sold.*

www.SilhouetteBombshell.com

SBIR

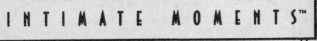

Silhouette®

INTIMATE MOMENTS™

CHARLIE SQUAD

NO MISSION IS TOO DANGEROUS
WHEN LIVES— AND LOVE—ARE ON THE LINE.

Rules of Engagement for Joe Rodriguez:

Rule 1: Remember, Carina Ferrare is the daughter of Charlie Squad's nemesis.

Rule 2: To rescue Carina you must marry her...and share her bed.

Rule 3: Forget everything you've ever believed about not falling in love with your work.

AVAILABLE MAY 2006 WHEREVER YOU BUY BOOKS.

HER ENEMY PROTECTOR

BY CINDY DEES

Visit Silhouette Books at www.eHarlequin.com   SIMHEP

$\blacktriangledown$ *Silhouette*®

SPECIAL EDITION™

Bound by fate, a shattered family renews
their ties—and finds a legacy of love.

Family
BUSINESS

HER
BEST-KEPT
SECRET

by Brenda Harlen

Jenny Anderson had always known
she was adopted. But a fling-turned-serious
with Hanson Media Group attorney
Richard Warren brought her closer than ever
to the truth about her past. In his arms,
would she finally find the love she's
always dreamed of?

Available in May 2006
wherever Silhouette books are sold.

Visit Silhouette Books at www.eHarlequin.com   SSEHBKS

If you enjoyed what you just read,
then we've got an offer you can't resist!

Take 2 bestselling
love stories FREE!

Plus get a FREE surprise gift!

Clip this page and mail it to Silhouette Reader Service®

IN U.S.A.	IN CANADA
3010 Walden Ave.	P.O. Box 609
P.O. Box 1867	Fort Erie, Ontario
Buffalo, N.Y. 14240-1867	L2A 5X3

YES! Please send me 2 free Silhouette Bombshell™ novels and my free surprise gift. After receiving them, if I don't wish to receive any more, I can return the shipping statement marked cancel. If I don't cancel, I will receive 4 brand-new novels every month, before they're available in stores! In the U.S.A., bill me at the bargain price of $4.69 plus 25¢ shipping & handling per book and applicable sales tax, if any*. In Canada, bill me at the bargain price of $5.24 plus 25¢ shipping & handling per book and applicable taxes**. That's the complete price and a savings of 10% off the cover prices—what a great deal! I understand that accepting the 2 free books and gift places me under no obligation ever to buy any books. I can always return a shipment and cancel at any time. Even if I never buy another book from Silhouettte, the 2 free books and gift are mine to keep forever.

200 HDN D34H
300 HDN D34J

Name	(PLEASE PRINT)	
Address	Apt.#	
City	State/Prov.	Zip/Postal Code

Not valid to current Silhouette Bombshell™ subscribers.
Want to try another series?
Call 1-800-873-8635 or visit www.morefreebooks.com.

* Terms and prices subject to change without notice. Sales tax applicable in N.Y.
** Canadian residents will be charged applicable provincial taxes and GST.
All orders subject to approval. Offer limited to one per household.
® and ™ are registered trademarks owned and used by the trademark owner and or its licensee.

BOMB04   ©2004 Harlequin Enterprises Limited

Silhouette® BOMBSHELL™

The Marian priestesses were destroyed long ago,
but their daughters live on. The time has come
for the heiresses to learn of their legacy, to unite
the pieces of a powerful mosaic and bring light to
a secret their ancestors died to protect.

The Madonna Key

Follow their quests each month.

COMING NEXT MONTH

#89 THE SPY WITH THE SILVER LINING—Wendy Rosnau
Spy Games

Chic superspy Casmir Balasi had played the game too well this time—getting love-struck master criminal Yuri Petrov to propose on bended knee…and fall into her trap. But when he escaped prison and vowed to enforce the "'til death do us part" clause of their sham marriage, all Casmir had for protection was her arrogant if irresistible bodyguard. Would her protector's secret agenda lead her into the hands of the enemy? Or into his arms?

#90 LOOK-ALIKE—Meredith Fletcher
Athena Force

Agent Elle St. John's loyalty to Russia clashed with her twin sister Sam's to America, but they were on the same team when it came to finding the truth behind their spy parents' deaths. Scouring Europe for clues—and fighting her attraction to the shadowy German helping her—Elle soon discovered a web of deceit entwining her parents, an Athena Academy blackmailer and security secrets from both twins' homelands.

#91 NO SAFE PLACE—Judy Fitzwater

When her estranged husband's dead body turned up—not once, but twice!—Elizabeth Larocca knew his dangerous secret life had caught up with him…and was about to catch up with her. So she took her grown daughter and ran. But her husband's associates were after her, men whose offers of help came across more as threats. Trusting no one, Elizabeth's only hope was to solve her husband's murder—and maybe prevent her own….

#92 INVISIBLE RECRUIT—Mary Buckham
IR-5

Jet-setter Vaughn Monroe needed a change. Why not try spying on for size? After all, her daddy was the CIA director. But it was tough joining the IR Agency, a group of covert women operatives, because her instructor mistook the debutante for dilettante. She proved him wrong—using connections to access a sinister private auction in India that other agencies couldn't infiltrate. Now, the fate of millions rested on Vaughn's next move….